1

'I need a new situation now,' Julia Marsh said, pushing aside the teacups and spreading the contents of her purse on the small table beside her. 'Look, two pounds, six shillings and threepence — and don't let's forget the half-penny, that will make a tremendous difference!'

'You need a husband,' her sister Fanny, Lady Cunningham, said briskly. 'You had your chances during your Season.'

Julia shuddered. 'Only desperate old men wanting a nurse or a mother for broods of children offered for a girl with no dowry, dependent on her sister and her rather unwilling brother-in-law for the very clothes she stood up in. If I have to be a nurse or governess I prefer to do it for a wage, and to be able to walk away if the people are uncongenial.'

She glanced down at her dull gown, at least two years out of date. It was appropriate for a companion to elderly ladies, being pale grey with no trimmings, and not very fashionable. Fanny wore a gown in a pretty pale apple-green, trimmed with darker green ruffles and braid. It suited her blonde fairness to perfection, and would have looked equally good with her own slightly darker honey-blonde hair. But she did not envy Fanny the husband who paid for such finery.

'Frederick was not unwilling,' Fanny said, but her tone was doubtful. 'He did rather hope you would become respectably established, though.'

Julia smiled. 'Well, I had an offer to become unrespectably established,' she said, and chuckled. 'What would your starchy Frederick have said if I'd accepted that?'

Fanny frowned. 'Your flippancy does not help. Will you apply for another post as companion?'

Julia sighed faintly. Poor Fanny had no sense of humour. She shook her head. 'I'm bored with reading tedious books of sermons to old ladies, and taking their irritating dogs for strolls in Sydney Gardens. I'm tired of Bath. I prefer the country, in any event, so I thought I'd apply for a position as governess. Young children would be a pleasant change. I have seen two advertisements today, and written letters. I'm praying I'll find something before you have to leave Greystones Manor.'

'You can stay here,' Fanny offered.

She was always kind, but she clearly hadn't considered what her husband would say

Marina Oliver has published over fifty novels and several non-fiction books on writing and local history and is a former chairman of the Romantic Novelists' Association. She divides her time between England and Madeira. For more details, see her website at: www.marina-oliver.net

THE ACCIDENTAL MARRIAGE

Julia goes with her sister Fanny and her husband Sir Frederick to Vienna, as governess to their daughters. There, the congress that is to settle the fate of Europe after the Napoleonic wars is gathering. Julia meets Sir Carey Evelegh, who has left his fiancée, Angelica, behind in England, with plans to return for a spring wedding. When Fanny sets off for home, Julia and her maid follow in another coach. But an accident on the way causes Julia to lose all her belongings. Now penniless, and a long way from home, who will help her to resolve her problem?

MARINA OLIVER

THE ACCIDENTAL MARRIAGE

Complete and Unabridged

ULVERSCROFT
Leicester

First published in Great Britain in 2008 by
Robert Hale Limited
London

First Large Print Edition
published 2009
by arrangement with
Robert Hale Limited
London

The moral right of the author has been asserted

British Library CIP Data

Oliver, Marina, *1934-*
    The accidental marriage
    1. British- -Austria- -Vienna- -Fiction.
    2. British- -Germany- -Bavaria- -Fiction.
    3. Bavaria (Germany)- -Social life and customs- -
    19th century- -Fiction. 4. Vienna (Austria)- -Social
    life and customs- -19th century- -Fiction. 5. Love
    stories. 6. Large type books.
    I. Title
    823.9′14−dc22

    ISBN 978−1−84782−708−1

Published by
F. A. Thorpe (Publishing)
Anstey, Leicestershire

Set by Words & Graphics Ltd.
Anstey, Leicestershire
Printed and bound in Great Britain by
T. J. International Ltd., Padstow, Cornwall

This book is printed on acid-free paper

about keeping his house open for the sake of an indigent sister-in-law. 'No, I can't stay here on my own. You'll want to close the house. You'll be away for several months.'

'I meant at the Dower House. It's not been used since Frederick's mother died last year, but the Harpers are there, they can easily look after you, until you find a suitable position. You mustn't take the first one that offers if it isn't what you'd like.'

Julia shrugged. She'd have to find something soon, whether it was what she wanted or no. Her last employer had been kind, and had promised to leave her some money, but she had died before changing her will, and her son declared he had no obligation for his mother's promises, if indeed she had made them, he'd added with a sneer.

Even a few pounds would have permitted her to take her time while seeking another post. She disliked being beholden to Sir Frederick Cunningham, who always gave the impression of disapproving of her. Perhaps this was because she was so very different from Fanny, who was gentle and pliable, always ready to believe Frederick knew best.

'How long does it take to travel to Vienna?' she asked, to change the subject.

'Three or four weeks, I expect. Probably more. It rather depends on how well the girls travel. We haven't ever taken them more than a dozen miles from home, and I'm dreading them developing travel sickness, and becoming bored and fretful. Thank goodness we have Miss Clarence to help keep them occupied.'

Julia gathered the coins together and slid them back into her purse. 'Do you have to take them?'

'It's an opportunity, now that odious Boney is safely locked away on Elba. Frederick wants to go to the Congress, and his grandmother has not seen the children. She wrote to say she hoped she would do so before she died. She is over seventy, so I suppose that's natural. And I've never met her either. But it seems a long way to go for just a few weeks. Frederick says the Congress will only last a month or two.'

'Why is he so anxious to go?'

'You know he has political ambitions. He feels that with so many rulers and ministers there he might find patronage.'

Julia did not reply. She had no great faith in her brother-in-law's political acumen, which she considered less than her own, and thought his chances of impressing someone with influence were remote. But Fanny loved and believed in him, and Julia, knowing her sister's lack of confidence, tried not to

4

criticize Frederick too often. Fanny was pretty, but far too self-effacing for Julia, who frequently had to bite her tongue in an attempt not to annoy Frederick. If he felt offended by her he was liable to complain to Fanny, saying she ought to control her sister better.

Fanny went on, her voice wistful. 'If times had been normal when we married, we'd probably have gone to visit her on our wedding journey, but the war was starting again, Europe wasn't safe.' She sighed. 'I've been a disappointment to Frederick. I just wish we'd had a son.'

Julia nodded. In nine years of marriage Fanny had produced only two girls, and after several miscarriages it seemed unlikely she would ever provide him with an heir. She knew Frederick blamed his wife. He frequently made fretful remarks about the lack of a son to inherit his title. Julia blamed him, for he spent a great deal of his time in London while Fanny was left alone in Hampshire, moping. On the one occasion she'd had the opportunity to observe him there, during her unsuccessful Season three years ago, she had been astonished, and then disgusted, at the manner in which he had neglected his wife in order to pay lavish attentions to other ladies. When she had protested to Fanny, her sister had merely said it was fashionable, it was not serious, and married couples did not sit in each other's pockets. Sometimes, Julia thought, Fanny seemed younger than she was, despite the six years' difference in their ages. If she ever married, which seemed unlikely, she would not tolerate such inconsiderate behaviour from a husband, whatever the fashionable world might say.

★ ★ ★

Within a week Julia received replies to her applications. Both said she was too young for the responsibility of caring for their children. She fumed. She would be one and twenty just before Christmas, less than five months away.

'They are probably afraid you're too pretty,' Fanny said, trying to console her. 'As well as the husbands, there are bound to be young male relatives who are susceptible to female charms.'

'And one of them might want to marry me,' Julia said, and laughed. 'I'll have to resign myself to being a companion again.'

It would be difficult, she admitted to herself an hour later, as she sat in her room and tried to compose yet another letter of application. This was to a lady of advanced years who needed a genteel companion with the ability to play the pianoforte, a clear speaking voice, a love of and patience with cats, and good French, for she would be required to write many letters to the lady's numerous correspondents all over Europe. At least the lady lived in Cheltenham, which would be a pleasant change from Bath.

Would she be expected to groom numerous cats? If they were anything like the vicarage cats she had known before her parents died, they would undoubtedly object with both tooth and claw. She must remember to acquire some thick leather gauntlets. No doubt Fanny would have an old pair. Perhaps she could become a schoolmistress? She shuddered. One or two young children would be tolerable, but cooped up in some academy containing a whole group of girls with little interest in anything but their own forthcoming Seasons, and marriage prospects, would drive her to distraction. If only respectable girls could have careers like their brothers! They could not become lawyers, or clergymen, or Members of Parliament. To have real influence, women had to be married to judges or bishops or be political hostesses, and her chances of living that sort of life were nil.

Meanwhile, she had reluctantly agreed to move into the Dower House. Fanny was unhappy at leaving her alone, with no one but the servants, but Julia insisted it would only be for a short while, until she found a position.

'I'll ask the rector's wife to keep an eye on you,' Fanny said.

Julia bit back her retort that she didn't want that inquisitive busybody poking her nose in where she wasn't welcome. Fanny was trying to do what she thought best for her sister. Julia had not told her of the disparaging comments Mrs Cleeve had made when she had seen Julia riding through the village unaccompanied by a groom. It had not satisfied her to be told that there was no groom available, and the errand she was undertaking for Fanny had been urgent.

She thought back to Fanny's remark that she needed a husband. Perhaps, and she grinned at the notion, she should advertise in the papers. Wanted, one handsome, kind, faithful, and preferably rich bachelor who would take to wife a stubborn, managing and moderately pretty girl with no dowry, but a clear speaking and singing voice, fluent French and some German and Italian.

Sighing, she reread the letter, picked up a wafer and sealed it. There could be no reply until after Fanny had left, the day after tomorrow. She glanced round the room. She had already taken most of her belongings, which were few, to the Dower House. She ought to gather up the rest and take them there now. She planned to move in today, wanting to know whether the plan would work, or whether there were unforeseen problems which might need sorting out before Fanny and Frederick departed.

She was carrying a valise downstairs when she heard raised voices in the small parlour where Fanny spent most of her time.

'I can't do it! I won't be cooped up in a stuffy, uncomfortable carriage for weeks!'

'But we offered you extra money,' Fanny said. 'You agreed!'

'I hadn't thought about it enough. I'm sorry, but I won't go.'

'How on earth will I find another governess in time?'

'I don't know. Perhaps you'll have to look after the children yourself for once!'

Julia stood aside as Miss Clarence, her colour high, and her hair in disarray as though she'd dragged her fingers through the normally demure bun, almost ran from the room, slamming the door behind her. Stifling a sob, and shrugging off Julia's outstretched hand, she ran up the stairs.

Julia looked back at the parlour door, set down her valise on the chequered marble floor and walked thoughtfully across the hall.

'I will almost certainly be back within three months, my sweet, in plenty of time for our wedding.'

Sir Carey Evelegh took the hand of the remarkably lovely girl who sat on the bench beside him, weeping bitterly, but when he tried to pull her towards him she snatched her hand away and stamped her foot.

'I don't want you to go!' she sobbed. 'If you truly loved me, you'd stay here. You don't know what it's like; Mama is always asking me silly questions, but whenever I tell her what I want in my trousseau she says it's not suitable, and I'm so tired of all the silly details! Why can't we just go to Gretna Green and avoid all this dreadful fuss!'

He laughed fondly, captured her hand again, and began to stroke the back of it with his fingers. How young she was, despite her usual air of sophistication. She'd been surrounded by eager suitors the moment she appeared in London. She was pretty, of good family, and had an ample dowry. When he himself, having been abroad during the spring, reached London in June, and she had shown an instant preference for him despite having received a couple of excellent offers, he had fallen under her spell. She was young, but would become an admirable wife and companion.

She shivered, and gave him a watery but apologetic glance, before moving closer to him and letting him put his arm round her waist. He breathed in the heady, intoxicating perfume she favoured.

'You'll enjoy the wedding. All girls do, and you'll look so beautiful, darling Angelica.'

She blinked. 'We could have been married by now, and I could have come with you.'

'Sweetheart, we only became betrothed a month ago; there just hasn't been time. Besides, a spring wedding will be lovely, and we can go on our wedding journey in the best weather.'

'We'll miss the Season.'

'Only the start of it, and there will be plenty more, for the rest of our lives. Time will pass quickly, I promise. And I really do have to go. Lord Castlereagh is taking the usual diplomats, and various clerks from the Foreign Office, but he wants other people there who can advise him. I spent some time in Poland and Russia a few years ago; I met the Tsar, and I think I can help.'

Angelica pouted, but permitted him to kiss her cheek. 'How long?' she asked.

'I'll travel as fast as I can, you may be sure. Especially on the way home. The Congress opens officially in October, and should be over by Christmas at the very latest.'

'But it's only the middle of August now!' Angelica interrupted. 'You need not go for a month or so. Why do you have to set off tomorrow?'

'Most of the important people will be there weeks beforehand, planning and organizing. I'm needed.'

It took time and patience, but eventually he was able to take his leave. He rode back to Courtlands, his home several miles away, trying to forget Angelica's mournful face as she waved farewell. His thoughts turned to the forthcoming negotiations in Vienna, the settlement the many interested countries were hoping to achieve now that Napoleon was finally defeated. His specially built travelling coach was ready, and he would set out early the next morning.

* * *

'I don't know what Frederick will say,' Fanny said, frowning.

'Surely he will prefer you to be freed from looking after the girls, so that you can help him.'

'It's not that. I don't suppose we will go out a great deal, or do much entertaining. Frau Gunter has a very small apartment, I believe. It's more that he would not want it known that his sister-in-law was employed in a menial position.'

Julia laughed. 'As to that, does he need to inform people I am your sister?'

Fanny shook her head vehemently. 'I won't disown you! Besides, if Frederick is busy, it would be pleasant to have your company if we do go to any entertainments. Maggie can share in looking after the girls, but she can't teach them as you could.'

'So it's agreed? I come with you.'

'If Frederick is willing.'

'Fanny, I'm fully aware he does not like me — '

'No, that's not true.'

Julia laughed. 'Oh, I grant it's not all personal. You had a portion left you by your godfather, so were acceptable as a wife. My godparents, however, have been inconsiderate enough to stay alive and look like surviving for many more years, they're so disgustingly healthy! So I have no expectations, and as such am an embarrassment to him. Don't worry, I have no desire for him to find me a husband.'

'But that would be an ideal solution.' Fanny was still wedded to that notion, however much Julia tried to convince her it was not her wish.

Julia admitted to herself she would welcome a husband, since the prospect of endlessly teaching small children, or ministering to the crotchets of elderly ladies, did not appeal as a lifelong occupation. But she was realistic. Without a portion, virtually penniless as she was, no sensible man would wish to marry her. So she might as well stop thinking about the possibility.

'I'll have no other chance of travelling,' she reminded Fanny. 'It would be a wonderful experience. You saw some of the important people in London earlier in the year. I'd love to see the Tsar, and his dreadfully vulgar sister, as well as the Emperor, and all the others. Besides, I speak some German, which might be of use to you.'

'Then you must come, whatever Frederick says. He'll have to see the sense of it. We must pay you what we pay Miss Clarence. More, perhaps, to compensate for the inconvenience of living in strange surroundings, and having to keep the children happy and occupied during the journey.'

Momentarily Julia quailed at this thought, but she liked her nieces, they were well-behaved children, and they always seemed happy in her company. It would not be too onerous a task to keep them amused. Better than grooming resentful cats. She had begun to give them lessons on the pianoforte, and teach them simple songs which they delighted in singing to their parents. She'd have gone without a salary, but she recognized the justice of being paid. She would be able to save most of it, which would help her on her return, enable her to take her time looking for a new position.

'We'd better tell Frederick now, in case he has any objections, and then I will get my things from the Dower House and start packing my trunk.'

* * *

Sir Carey breathed a deep sigh as he surveyed the small two-room apartment he had rented in a narrow street close to St Stephen's Cathedral. The journey had taken three weeks, and he was heartily weary of the undiluted company of Tanner, his valet, whose only conversation had been a polite 'yes, sir', or 'indeed, sir', and very occasionally, 'is that so, sir?' Tanner and Frisby, his coachman, would share a small attic room on the upper floor. Neither of them had looked pleased at this arrangement, but there were so many visitors in Vienna they had been fortunate to get a room at all.

Lord Castlereagh had not yet arrived, but

was expected within days. Sir Carey left Tanner unpacking his gear and strolled out to get his bearings, and perhaps meet some acquaintances.

Vienna, he discovered, was a maze of narrow streets, a jumble of aristocratic mansions side by side with the lesser houses of the merchants, many of whom appeared to live above their shops or restaurants, and the buildings which housed the poorer citizens. Constrained by the ramparts of the old city walls, the people of Vienna had built upwards. Though this, and the narrowness of the streets, kept the sunlight out for much of the time, there were many squares and open spaces, most of them filled with trees, so the city did not feel claustrophobic.

Returning to his apartment, having seen no one he knew, he paused for a glass of wine in a café near the Hofburg Palace. Sir Carey thought he had never seen so many cafés, restaurants and shops in such a small space. All were doing excellent business, for the city was crammed with thousands of visitors from all over Europe and Russia, and this was before the main delegations had arrived. The Viennese would be having a profitable time, he mused, and maybe it was necessary. The Emperor Francis would need to increase taxation to pay for the lavish entertainments

Sir Carey had heard were being planned.

He returned to his room and sat down to write to Angelica, a tender smile on his face. Though her family lived only a dozen miles from Courtlands, they moved in different circles in the country, and he hadn't seen her since she was a child. When she had accepted him, instead of some far more eligible men who had been paying her serious attentions, he had been overwhelmed with an amazed gratitude. She was the prettiest debutante of the Season, had sufficient fortune not to have to marry for money, and she had a gentle disposition. She had seemed to cling to him from the start, probably finding comfort in the fact they came from the same county. He thought himself the happiest of men, and spared a few moments pitying the wealthier or higher born men she had rejected.

It had been a severe wrench to insist their wedding be delayed until after his return from the Congress. Angelica did not care for a great show, she'd insisted, and would have willingly accompanied him to Vienna. He had been afraid that if she did not have the sort of wedding most girls wished for, she would in later years regret it. And much as he would have relished her company on this mission, he knew her presence would have prevented him from doing a competent job.

17

* ★ *

Fanny bit her lip, and glanced from under her eyelashes at Julia, who was regarding the hands clasped together in her lap with fixed attention. She could have sworn her sister was desperately suppressing a laugh.

Frau Gunter was of the old school, still rigidly upright and tightly corseted. She wore the elaborate embroidered and panniered dresses of the last century, a powdered wig, and used a great deal of cosmetics on her wizened face.

They had arrived before noon, having spent the previous night at an inn outside the city, but Frau Gunter had kept to her own room until just before the dinner hour, and they met her only when sipping inferior sherry before the meal.

Her first words had been disapproving comments about the light muslins Fanny and Julia wore, and she expressed the pious hope that their behaviour would not be as slight or indecorous as their appearances promised. Then she had turned to the children, who were looking terrified, and noted with approval on their resemblance to Frederick.

'I thought they resembled my mother,' Fanny said quietly, emboldened to this mild rebellion by the presence of Julia. Her sister, though occasionally causing her perturbation, was usually a welcome support.

Frau Alice Gunter snorted. 'They may be insipid blondes,' she said in guttural French, 'but they have the Gunter nose, just as Frederick's mother did. It's a pity he did not inherit it. It looks better on a man.'

Julia uttered a choking sound, disguised as a cough, and Frau Gunter turned to her.

'Do you have a cold?' she asked. 'If so, I would be pleased if you keep yourself away from me. I cannot afford to take risks at my age.'

'No, ma'am, I am perfectly well,' Julia replied cheerfully. 'But I will certainly keep out of your way as much as possible. I mean to teach the children all I can about Vienna and history while we are fortunate to be living here, so I will be taking them out to see the city whenever the weather is clement enough.'

Frau Gunter looked hard at her, then sniffed, and Fanny bit her lip again. She was tempted to ask if the old lady had a cold, but knew she would have to keep silence if their stay was to be bearable.

It would be difficult, Fanny thought. She and Frederick had been allocated the smallest bedroom in the apartment, while Julia, her maid, Maggie, Frau Gunter's maid, Ilse, and the two girls shared a slightly larger one.

There was just one salon, where it would be impossible to give dinner parties, as it was large enough to hold a dozen people at most. Frederick's valet, Silvers, and the coachman, Evans, had been relegated to a tiny room off the even tinier kitchen, which was normally used as a storeroom for preserves and an accumulation of old furniture, trunks, and several piles of books and old copies of the *Weiner Zeitung*. There had just been room, Frederick had grumpily reported, after piling things to one side, for a narrow palliasse the men would have to share.

'Silvers will give notice,' he'd predicted. 'I'll find us somewhere more suitable tomorrow.'

Fanny wished he had been able to. But after several hours he had returned to say there was just no suitable accommodation available, there were so many visitors to the city. They would have to endure the crowding, and the disagreeable attitude of his grandmother.

They escaped as soon as dinner was over, saying that after the journey they needed an early night.

'What an unpleasant woman!' Julia whispered.

Fanny nodded. 'Let's hope the Congress is soon over. I don't think I can endure much of this. Frederick said Lord Castlereagh arrived yesterday. It's two weeks to the official opening, and perhaps four weeks for the negotiations. I'm already counting the days.'

'We must get out as much as possible. Let's take the girls exploring tomorrow morning. I saw several parks as we drove in, and Ilse says they are all open to everyone.'

2

Julia smiled as the children ran on ahead, Paula screaming to her sister to wait for her. After three weeks cooped up in the travelling carriage, with their father frowning whenever they made a noise, Alice and Paula were only too willing to explore Vienna's many parks. Frau Gunter had been more amenable this morning, possibly because she partook of breakfast in bed, and only encountered the children when they were on their way out.

'She was almost friendly,' Fanny said, as they strolled along the chestnut-bordered paths in the Prater. 'It may not be so bad after all. I suspect it was the shock of all of us descending on her yesterday.'

'She'd invited you to stay,' Julia said. 'She must have known how many of us there are, unless she didn't think you'd bring any servants.'

'I don't suppose she bothered to count. But she told Frederick last night that a friend of hers with a larger apartment was thinking of leaving Vienna and going to Salzburg to stay with her son while the Congress is here. We might be able to rent that. He's grumbling at the expense, but he's willing to pay in order to have more space and our own rooms for entertaining. He's already been invited to several receptions and balls, and he says there will be even more once the other delegations arrive.'

'I thought the Congress was for talking,' Julia began, but was interrupted by a howl from Paula, who had tripped over her feet as she looked backwards at some soldiers exercising their horses. A group of horses ridden by ladies was trotting towards her, only yards away and, as she rolled over, she was directly in their path.

By the time Fanny and Julia reached the little girl she had been scooped out of danger and set on her feet by a man passing by.

'I don't think she's hurt, ma'am,' he said, smiling at Fanny, as Paula clung to her skirts, sobbing.

'Paula, dear, let me look at your knees,' Fanny said. 'Did you scrape them?'

Alice came running back, and grasped Julia's hand. She reassured the little girl that Paula wasn't badly hurt, and turned to the man, smiling ruefully. 'Thank you, sir. I shouldn't have been letting them run about, but they are so pleased to be out of the coach.'

He was, she noted, very personable and

impeccably, even expensively dressed. Tall, with dark wavy hair, and piercing blue eyes, he was a man who would have attracted attention in any gathering. And he had a devastating smile.

'You have come out from England?' he asked now. 'I arrived a few days ago, and I am still aching from the jolting. Let me introduce myself. Sir Carey Evelegh, at your service.'

'I'm Julia Marsh, and this is my sister, Lady Cunningham. And her daughters, Alice and Paula.'

Alice shyly held out her hand, and Paula, prompted by Fanny, did the same. She gulped, and with a watery smile said a quiet 'thank you.'

'We're in your debt, Sir Carey,' Fanny said. 'I was expecting her to be trampled on.'

'No, there was plenty of room, the horses would have avoided her. Is your husband Sir Frederick Cunningham? I have met him occasionally in London, and he mentioned he was coming here.'

'Do come and call,' Fanny invited. 'He will be happy to see a friend. We may not be at this address for more than a few days, though, we hope to move into a larger apartment.'

'I would be delighted. Enjoy the rest of your walk, ladies. Goodbye, Alice and Paula, I hope to see you again soon.'

He raised his hat and walked away.

Julia looked after him. 'What do you hazard he'll forget all about us?' she asked. 'He didn't say Frederick was his friend. Has Frederick ever mentioned him?'

'No, but he doesn't tell me about his London cronies. Wasn't he handsome? I wonder whether he is married?'

Julia laughed. 'Fanny, I beg you, don't start matchmaking here. I'm your children's governess, remember!'

'Stuff and nonsense. You're my sister. I hope he does call.'

★   ★   ★

To Fanny's delight Frau Schwartz, Frau Gunter's friend, agreed to let them rent her apartment, which was in the next building, as well as her cook and housemaid to look after them.

'It has six whole rooms!' she told Julia. 'There are two salons, connected by double doors, so we can entertain properly.'

Julia thought of Greystones, the rambling, many-roomed Jacobean manor house that was Fanny's home, and the London house they rented when they spent the Season there. Two salons seemed quite inadequate, unless they were spacious. She suspected they would not, in the end, do a great deal of entertaining. From rumours they had heard the official receptions, balls, military reviews, shooting and hunting parties, together with the theatrical performances, concerts and ballets, would fully occupy the time. She could not imagine when the ministers would find time for negotiations, unless they did it over the card and supper tables.

By the following day they were installed, and when Sir Carey called two days afterwards, having been given their new direction by Frau Gunter, Fanny was able to welcome him in a large, ornately furnished drawing-room.

'We hear the ministers are already talking,' Fanny said. 'Are they not waiting for the other delegations to arrive?'

'They are discussing how to go about it, which we hope will save time once the Congress opens officially. Have you received invitations to the reception at the Hofburg, on the thirtieth?'

'Frederick hasn't said.'

'There is also a masked ball two days later, after the regimental parade. Everyone will be going to that. Even a palace as huge as the Hofburg will be crowded. It's a vast place, like a city. It's been added to over the

26

centuries as the Hapsburgs gained more power. The oldest part is thirteenth century, but for the rest, all sorts of styles, rather like my own home but on a far grander scale. I will hope to see you there, but in such a crush who knows whether we'll meet?'

'Oh, we didn't bring dominoes and masks,' Fanny said.

'Then we had better go shopping tomorrow,' Julia said briskly. 'What other entertainments are planned, Sir Carey? Surely they won't all be huge affairs?'

He grinned, and she felt a slight fluttering sensation in the region of her heart. He really was enormously attractive.

'All the ministers will be entertaining. I hear Metternich has something very grand arranged.'

'We heard that the Princess Bagration is giving a ball the day after the reception, but Frederick said that is a small affair. We saw her yesterday, out driving in the Prater. She is amazingly pretty. She's Russian, is she not?'

'She's related to the Tsar. Tell me, were you in London during the celebrations in the summer when he visited? I saw Sir Frederick there once or twice, but we did not meet, Lady Cunningham.'

As Fanny began to describe what she had seen, and deplore the massive crowds that had been everywhere, hoping for glimpses of the Tsar and the other important visitors, Julia frowned slightly. Why had he changed the subject so abruptly?

'What's the matter with Princess Bagration?' she demanded, after he had left.

Fanny shook her head. 'I haven't a notion. But he did not want to talk about her, did he? Perhaps he's in love with her. After all, he did say he'd spent some time in Russia, so he probably met her there.'

'We'll no doubt discover it soon enough. Maggie says the servants spend half their time gossiping, when they are supposed to be marketing. I imagine their employers do too! Do we go and shop for your domino this afternoon, or wait until morning?'

'Yours, too. You'll have to come with me. Frederick won't want to have to stay beside me all night, and I'd be terribly nervous on my own.'

Julia did not protest. As well as recognizing the truth of Fanny's words, she was eager to see Emperor Francis's Hofburg Palace from the inside. They had seen the outside the previous day when they had been exploring the old quarter of the city. And she admitted to herself the hope that she might achieve a waltz with Sir Carey. This dance, which so many in England considered shocking, was much more popular on the Continent, and she had secretly learned how to dance it from a friend she had made in Bath, a niece of her late employer who had wanted a partner to practise with before she went to London for her first Season.

*   *   *

Sir Carey was writing a letter to Angelica, but found his attention distracted by thoughts of the problems he could foresee arising in Vienna. Prince Talleyrand had arrived, accompanied by Dorothée de Corlande, wife of his nephew, who acted as his official hostess, and objected vehemently to what he saw as an attempt by the four powers of Austria, Britain, Prussia and Russia to settle matters between themselves. Eventually the letter was very brief, describing his doings in the two days since he had last written to her. It was time to prepare for the masked ball.

The Hofburg Palace, when he arrived, was sumptuously decorated in red and gold. Such was the crowd of people arriving he was late, and entered the Redoutensalle to see the Tsar, that unpredictable man who had created such offence in London by his rudeness, leading the Austrian Empress in a stately polonaise. He joined the throng which went up the grand staircase, through various rooms, and came finally to the Audience Chamber.

He hadn't been here before, and gazed round in awe. It was huge, with golden pillars and hangings of red velvet. Most of the guests appeared to be equally impressed, whether they were minor German royalty or plebeian merchants who rarely had the opportunity of mingling with so many aristocrats.

After a while he began to wander through the maze of rooms, sampling the food from the many buffets, but looking for the English family he had encountered. He told himself they would be overwhelmed. They were not of the level of society which attended the Prince Regent's lavish entertainments at Carlton House. Indeed, when he had mentioned them, Fanny had shuddered and declared she never wished to be invited. It had been a sufficient ordeal when she was presented during her first Season.

The dominoes, disguising figures to some extent, apart from when the wearers were whirling in the dances, made it difficult to recognize people, though the masks were small enough to allow people who knew each other well to find their friends. He was estimating his chances of finding Lady Cunningham and her party as exceedingly remote when he heard Julia's voice. It was clear, musical, and distinctive.

He swung round, smiling. She was standing a few yards away, talking animatedly to a man he knew was a minor official at the Foreign Office, one of the clerks who had accompanied Lord Castlereagh. Fanny and Sir Frederick and an unknown couple were also in the group. Sir Frederick was looking grim.

'Good evening,' he said, moving towards them. 'Lady Cunningham, I hope you will do me the honour of dancing with me?'

She looked nervous, and glanced at her husband. Frederick forced a smile to his lips.

'My wife has promised me this dance,' he said abruptly.

'Then Miss Marsh, perhaps?' Sir Carey said smoothly. He could not suppress the feeling that she would be a much livelier companion than her sister, who appeared to be a rather timid, unconfident woman.

They looked alike, superficially, but Julia was taller, more slender, and had slightly darker, honey-coloured hair, and deeper blue, almost violet, eyes. She was more vivid in every way, in both looks and deportment.

Julia smiled and took his hand, and he led her towards the nearest ballroom, where the musicians were playing a waltz.

'Oh dear,' she said, and laughed. 'Frederick

will disapprove for days. He thinks the waltz is depraved. I doubt he'll dance it even with his wife. It was to prevent you from dancing with her that he claimed her hand.'

Sir Carey grinned. 'I don't suppose you will allow his disapproval to affect you.'

He placed his arm about her waist and swung her into the crowd of dancers. She was, as he'd expected, an excellent dancer, and they twirled about, dipping and swaying to the music.

'Heavens, no! I've suffered his displeasure ever since he met Fanny. I'm just thankful he doesn't expect me to live with them all the time.'

'You live with your parents?'

'My parents died five years ago. I lived with Fanny and Frederick until my come out, but when I didn't take — and how could I have done with no portion and no great beauty to compensate, like the Gunning sisters — I started to earn my living as a companion. I'm only here now because Fanny's governess declined to come at the last minute, and I was looking for a new position. You are dancing with a humble governess, sir!'

'Not so humble,' he retorted, laughing. 'So you are in charge of those delightful little girls. No doubt they prefer that to whatever governess they had before.'

'You, sir, are a flatterer,' she said. 'I wouldn't mind being a governess if all my charges were so clever and amenable. It would be a pleasant change from grooming dogs and cats.'

She gave an involuntary shiver, and his arm tightened about her waist.

'What do you mean?'

Julia laughed, and explained. 'I applied for a position where I would have been expected to groom cats. I have nothing against the creatures, apart from when they are being brushed and combed against their will.'

Sir Carey laughed. 'I have a cousin who spends all his money commissioning statues and paintings of his menagerie — or should I call it cattery? When I last heard, he had at least two dozen.'

He grew pensive, thinking of his cousin Daniel. He was wealthy, but a miser, spending as little as possible apart from his obsession with the felines. When he glanced at Julia she was eyeing him with a slight frown in her eyes, but she did not ask to be told his thoughts.

The waltz ended and they went back to where they had left Fanny and Frederick. They had disappeared, and reluctant to abandon Julia on her own in a crowd that was becoming boisterous, he suggested they found some food and glasses of wine.

The buffets were lavish, and they loaded plates and took them to a small side room which had been set with small tables.

It was half an hour before Fanny, looking flustered, found them. A pity, Sir Carey couldn't help thinking. Julia was an interesting companion, with sensible, firm views of her own, but he knew he had monopolized her company for too long.

'I trust we'll meet again soon,' he said, bowing himself away.

* * *

Fanny sank on to the chair he had vacated, and Julia looked closely at her.

'What's the matter?' she asked. 'Where's Frederick?'

'Oh, he's dancing. With some Russian girl, I understand. He said when we were introduced that he'd met her in London. I think she was something to do with the Tsar's sister, perhaps one of her ladies. But the Grand Duchess is not here, so I don't understand why she is.'

Julia suppressed a sigh. Frederick was clearly up to his old tricks, but it was scarcely gallant of him to have deserted Fanny, as he must have done, in such a large crowd. It would do no good complaining, however. Fanny needed to believe in him, and she herself had to live in harmony with him while they were in such circumscribed quarters.

'Do you want any food?' she asked instead. 'There are buffets in all the rooms, and I'll fetch you some if you wish.'

Fanny shook her head. 'Tell me about Sir Carey. Did you find out much about him?'

'Not a great deal, apart from the fact he has a cousin who is passionate about cats, and spends all his money on them.'

'I wonder if he is married?'

Julia frowned. 'He didn't say, but Fanny, please don't try to matchmake. If you pursue him too eagerly, you'll frighten him away.'

Fanny looked thoughtful. 'Yes, of course. You are right, and how sensible. We'll treat him carefully, just as a friend. And then we'll be able to find out his situation.'

What did it matter? Julia thought, grinding her teeth. Fanny was incorrigible, and nothing she could say would change her. Then she admitted, deep down, that the answer would interest her too. Not, she hastened to tell herself, that it could make any possible difference to her situation. Without a portion, she would never be able to marry anyone half as attractive as Sir Carey, and she had better make her mind up to it.

'I've found out about the Princess Bagration,'
Fanny announced, a few days later when she
returned from a shopping expedition. 'Her
husband was killed at Borodino, but she's had
dozens of lovers, including Metternich. They
call her the 'naked angel' because she cuts her
bodices indecently low. She and the Duchess
of Sagan both have apartments in the Palais
Palm, and apparently she is no better, and
what's more,' she added breathlessly, 'Metternich fell in love with her, and is distraught
because she has taken a new lover.'

Julia laughed. 'What a coil! Do you think
any real talking is happening? So far there
have been endless balls, and now they have
agreed to have a recess until November. The
Congress hasn't started properly. It seems it
will go on for months.'

Fanny sighed. 'I've decided we have to have
a small party. We've met several people now,
enough to fill the salons. There's the Pryces;
they're renting an apartment in this building,
and our nearest English neighbours. Then
Lord Pendle and his sister, and the Webbers.
They are dreadful gossips, of course, but they
are friendly with Frederick's grandmother,
and I suppose some people find them
amusing. And Sir Carey, we must invite him

too. Will you help me write invitations? I thought next Wednesday.'

To Fanny's relief most of the people accepted. She suggested Julia might teach the little girls simple songs they could sing for the guests.

'I'm not sure that's a good idea,' Julia said. 'They will be shy.'

'Of course they won't be too shy. They love to sing for our friends at home.'

'Yes, but these people will all be strangers.'

'Just simple English nursery rhymes. They already know several.'

Frederick had entered the room during this conversation, and nodded to Fanny.

'Of course, my dear. Julia, you are not saying you cannot manage the girls, are you?'

'They will do their best, but Paula is only four.'

'You must impress on them that it is important for them to make a good impression.'

Why? Julia wanted to ask. Then she understood. Frederick had insisted that Fanny invited the Russian Countess Tania with some unpronounceable title. Frederick no doubt wished to show off his children to his latest flirt.

* * *

37

The party was going well. The cook they had hired with the apartment had produced a magnificent buffet. Julia had been helping, pressed into service when the cook had protested at the work involved, saying darkly that her mistress never entertained on such a lavish scale. By judicious flattery Julia had worked out a menu, and when she promised to help, saying she would assist the maids with the tedious preparation, while the cook could demonstrate her skills with the more difficult aspects, the woman had been mollified.

Julia just had time, before the first guests arrived, to change into the new evening gown Fanny had insisted on buying for her. It was of a delicate apricot-coloured silk, the skirts gored and wider than had been fashionable. The neckline was low, but Julia had seen others, including Fanny's own, far lower. Instead of ruffles round the hem and the edges of the puff sleeves being of a darker shade, which is what Julia would have expected, hers were a pale cream, and she had pale cream sandals, plus a gauze scarf in a darker shade of apricot. Julia put on her only jewellery, a gold chain and simple gold ear-rings, and decided she did her sister proud. Would Sir Carey think so?

Fanny wanted the girls to display their

singing before the buffet, so that they could go to bed at their normal time. When the guests were assembled, all drinking champagne, Frederick called for silence, and Julia led the two little girls, dressed in pretty white dresses trimmed with artificial flowers, into the salon. She took up her position at the pianoforte, and giving a nod of encouragement to the girls, began to play.

Alice was to sing first. Julia thought that her example would encourage Paula, who was far more nervous. After a false start, during which Julia heard a quiet titter which she suspected came from the Countess Tania, Alice managed to sing Oranges and Lemons, without getting any of the names incorrectly, and retreated, blushing furiously, at the generous applause she received.

'Now, Paula,' Frederick announced.

Paula stepped forward, and Fanny moved to hold her hand, to give encouragement. The child was gulping nervously, and when Julia played the opening notes of Baa Baa Black Sheep, she turned away and hid her face in Fanny's lap.

'Try again,' Julia whispered, and Paula glanced up at her, bit her lip, and once more faced the audience.

She managed the first few words, and Julia, to encourage her, sang softly with her. It wasn't enough. Suddenly the child turned and weeping hysterically, ran from the room. Fanny jumped up but Julia was before her.

'I'll go to her. You must stay with your guests,' she said hurriedly, pushing Fanny round.

Over her sister's shoulder she glimpsed Frederick's furious face.

The guests had begun to talk to cover the momentary awkwardness, but Julia heard yet another titter. Furious, she stalked from the room, followed by a nervous Alice, and went to find and comfort Paula.

It was some time before the child, exhausted by her weeping, fell asleep. Julia considered going to bed herself, but knew Fanny would need her support. The buffet, which had, she was told by a nervous Fanny, been much appreciated, was finished, and Julia thought longingly of the delicacies she had intended to sample.

Some of the guests were getting ready to leave, but Sir Carey, who had been sitting at the far end of the salon while the girls had been performing, came up to Julia and smiled.

'Your own voice should have been entertaining us,' he said. 'It is very accomplished. You could earn your living with it if you had to.'

'It would certainly be preferable to grooming cats,' Julia said, laughing.

'Little Paula will overcome her shyness in time. She is too young to face so many strangers and be expected to perform.'

'That was what I told Fanny,' Julia said, 'but Frederick was determined to show them off.'

And furious, she discovered, when all the guests had departed. The last one had barely left the apartment when he turned on her and, ignoring Fanny's pleas to let it rest, berated her for Paula's exhibition.

'You should have prepared her better!' he raged. 'What a fiasco! What do you think our friends thought of such a display of temper?'

'Temper?' Julia repeated. 'That was not temper! Paula was devastated at the commotion she had caused, but you should never have insisted on her performing. If it was a fiasco it was your doing! But I'm sure most of your guests understood and were sympathetic. Apart from whoever it was who could not control her deplorable tittering.'

He went red, but after glaring at her stormed out of the room, and moments later they heard the outer door of the apartment slam.

Fanny began to cry. 'He's gone to her!' she sobbed. 'Julia, what shall I do?'

3

They had just finished breakfast, and Maggie had taken the girls away to start the lessons Julia had set them, when a visitor was announced.

It was Sir Carey. Julia found herself slightly breathless, and inwardly chastised herself. It was inappropriate. From his handsome clothes he was clearly affluent, and she was a penniless governess. Nonetheless, she wished she had put on one of the new gowns Fanny had insisted on buying her, instead of the old grey one.

'Forgive me, ladies, for calling at such an hour, but I have a meeting with Lord Castlereagh shortly. I wanted to reassure myself that little Paula is not too distressed after last night.'

Fanny smiled at him. 'How kind, Sir Carey. She is a little subdued, but Julia has given her some pictures to colour. It's her favourite occupation at the moment, and will take her mind off it.'

He smiled. 'All little girls seem to enjoy that. My sisters were for ever plaguing their governess to allow them such a treat, instead of doing sums.'

'How many sisters do you have?' Fanny asked.

'Two, half-sisters, aged twelve and fifteen. My father married again after my mother died. Unfortunately he and their mother died several years ago when there was an outbreak of cholera in the nearby town, so I am responsible for them.'

'You are married? Your wife must be a help to you,' Fanny said, and Julia shrivelled inside. How could her sister be so obvious?

Sir Carey was shaking his head. 'Not yet, Lady Cunningham, but I am to be wed in the spring, when I go back to England. Angelica is not very much older than my sister Caroline, and I am sure they will get on famously.'

It didn't matter to her in the least, Julia told herself firmly. How could such an attractive man not be married or betrothed. Even if he were free, there was no chance of him looking towards dowerless, insignificant Julia Marsh for a wife. She was being foolish even thinking of such a possibility. She felt a pang of envy for the unknown Angelica, and firmly suppressed it.

Sir Carey was rising to his feet. 'I must be going. No doubt I will see you both at the Peace Ball next Tuesday?'

'Yes, we will be there. Prince Metternich is

generous with his invitations. I hear he has over two hundred people to dine at the Chancellery every Monday.'

'Have you not been?'

Fanny shook her head. 'Frederick isn't in that strata of society,' she said wryly.

'We must see what we can do to get you invitations. Now, ladies, farewell.'

★　★　★

'What is it you are doing to drive Frederick into the arms of other women?' Frau Gunter demanded.

Julia stiffened, angered by the old woman's imperious tone. She glanced at Fanny, who shrank back into the chair, and looked as though she would burst into tears at any moment.

'I haven't done anything,' Fanny managed.

'Sit up straight! No wonder the girls are so undisciplined when you cannot even conduct yourself with proper decorum. I hear they made an unseemly commotion at your little party.'

Fanny was on the verge of tears, so Julia intervened, trying to keep the anger out of her voice.

'Alice sang beautifully, but it was too much strain for Paula, being forced to sing in front of so many strangers. She's only four! It's hardly surprising she found it impossible.'

'Only four, indeed! At that age I was conversing in German, French and Italian to my parents' visitors. And who asked you to contradict me? You are only the governess, and not a very good one at that if you cannot train the girls to behave with decorum.'

'They are not circus animals to be trained,' Julia said through gritted teeth. Really, this old woman was impossible. She needed someone to stand up to her. 'And if Frederick is making a fool of himself and causing talk, that is his doing, not ours. It's pathetic for a grown man to be in such a pet just because Paula cannot obey his idiotish commands!'

'How dare you speak to me in such a manner! Leave us. And if Fanny cares for my opinion she will dismiss you at once.'

Julia slowly rose to her feet, but instead of leaving the room she crossed to the bellpull and tugged it. Klara, the housemaid, entered, looking faintly scared.

'Frau Gunter is leaving, Klara. Please show her out.'

Frau Gunter opened her mouth to protest, but rose slowly to her feet. Julia suppressed a satisfied smile. It was clearly beneath her dignity to argue in front of the servants.

'You will regret this, Miss Marsh,' she said

as she went out of the room. 'Believe me, you will regret it.'

Fanny breathed a sigh of relief. 'Oh Julia, thank you! I would have been in floods of tears soon. That horrible old woman! How dare she blame us for Frederick's behaviour? But she will find a way of punishing us, and Frederick will no doubt blame me.'

'If you are on your own, deny her. Maggie's loyal to you, she'll say you are ill, and stay with you, and if you remain in your room she's hardly likely to force her way past Maggie. It's beneath her precious dignity.'

'Frederick is hoping she may leave the girls a legacy. She's very rich.'

Julia frowned at her sister. 'Frederick is not poor, he can well afford to give the girls whatever they need. And it's his behaviour at fault. He's seen everywhere with that wretched Tania, feeding the gossip. Though with all the other liaisons going on here, it's a wonder people have time to gossip about him.'

'He's being much more blatant than he is in London,' Fanny said, and sighed.

Julia looked at Fanny's drooping lips. 'Don't you really mind?' she asked gently.

A tear rolled down Fanny's cheek. 'Of course I mind! I love him, Julia. But everybody seems to do it; it's the fashion, so how can I complain?'

'I would, if it were my husband. Even if I didn't love him I'd be angry at the humiliation.'

Fanny took out a flimsy cambric handkerchief and wiped her eyes. 'It hurts, of course it does, but if I showed that in public people would laugh at me for being provincial and unsophisticated.'

'Does he know? Have you told him how you feel?'

'Yes, but he won't listen. He says I'm being ridiculous, and there's no more to it than him merely being pleasant and paying compliments to women, who all expect it.'

'Stuff and nonsense! Of course we all like being praised, but women who steal husbands away from their wives are nothing but trollops, however highly born they might be!'

She stopped abruptly. It would serve no purpose to tell Fanny what she thought men like Frederick should be called.

Fanny gave a small, stifled laugh. 'I've sometimes thought I should do the same, and find a man who will pay me the same sort of attentions.'

'And make Frederick jealous?'

'Yes,' Fanny sighed, 'but I can't do it. I can't flirt like that, so no man has ever suggested anything the least improper to me. Besides, I doubt Frederick would notice, or care if he did. He'd just think it gave him more licence.'

Julia wasn't so sure. In her admittedly limited experience, most men regarded their wives as possessions, and reacted like dogs over bones if they thought they were in danger of losing what they owned. She began to weave fantasies in which she encouraged her sister to show an interest in another man. Sir Carey was the obvious choice; he was the only single man — or betrothed, she hastily reminded herself — they knew as more than a passing acquaintance. But somehow the notion of flinging Fanny in his path did not appeal. And she was sure, she told herself, dismissing the idea, that neither he nor Fanny would co-operate.

★   ★   ★

Sir Carey returned to his lodgings later that day to find a letter from Angelica waiting for him. Smiling, he tore it open. It was only the third one from her, and he had concluded she was not a diligent correspondent. Caroline, the older of his sisters, was already an

48

assiduous letter-writer, and wrote to him almost every day, letters full of her and her sister Susan's doings, the gossip about people in the village, what the servants at Courtlands were doing, and letters she had received from her numerous correspondents, who seemed to include almost every member of her mother's family as well as many of her former schoolfriends. Sometimes he wondered how she ever found time to do her lessons and all the other activities she described in such detail.

Angelica's writing was still that of a schoolgirl, and her sentences stiff and formal. They showed none of the liveliness which had first drawn him to her. Had she been told what to write by Mrs Philpot, her rather formidable mother? Did that lady, who had only permitted them to be alone together for very brief periods after the betrothal was announced, consider correspondence between the happy pair needed to be supervised? Was she afraid too many expressions of regard, or even love, would contaminate her pure daughter? He thought ruefully of his own letters, which had contained warm sentiments looking forward to their happiness after they were finally together. No doubt her mother insisted on reading those.

It was good to hear from her, however

vaguely unsatisfactory he found the epistles. She had returned to London after a month in the country, mainly, she wrote, to purchase her trousseau and have fittings for her wedding gown.

She had heard something of the ceremony in Vienna, and asked him if he had seen the formal entry of the Emperor and the Tsar, and all the other kings and princes. Had they concluded the negotiations, and would he be coming home for Christmas? They had been invited to a large house party near York, and she would enjoy it so much more if he were there with her. She remained, his affectionate Angelica.

He put down the single sheet of paper, and wished he might be going home for Christmas, but from the slow progress of the negotiations it seemed highly unlikely. The big powers were locked in a seemingly intractable dispute about Poland. The Tsar, in occupation, wanted to maintain his influence. Castlereagh wanted a strong independent Poland as a buffer between Russia and Europe. King Frederick William of Prussia had promised Polish provinces to the Tsar in return for Saxony, which would upset the balance of power in Europe. Talleyrand was determined that France would not lose just because it had been dominated for so long by

Napoleon. The multitude of small German princes all wanted to improve their own positions, and the larger German duchies and principalities were vociferous in their own demands. How would they ever reconcile all these conflicting aims?

Sitting down at the table he wrote a swift and affectionate reply to Angelica, and then settled down to composing the report Castlereagh had asked for on conditions in Russia as he had known them four years ago, before Napoleon had sent his Grande Armée against the Tsar, with such disastrous consequences.

★ ★ ★

Julia was returning with the girls from their daily expedition to the Prater, when she met Mrs Pryce, who had an apartment in the same building. She greeted the children with big smiles, and to Julia's relief did not mention their singing the previous evening.

'Hello, children. Have you been for a walk? The weather is glorious, is it not? One can scarce believe it's the middle of October. Miss Marsh, could I prevail on you to permit Alice and Paula to come and play with my daughters? They're much of an age, and it would be good for all of them to have different company occasionally. I fear Amelia and Charlotte sometimes get fretful with one another, being thrown together so much. They miss their playmates at home.'

Alice turned hopeful eyes up to Julia. 'Oh, Aunt Julia, may we?'

'We must ask your mother, but I'm sure she'll agree. It's most kind of you, Mrs Pryce.'

'It will give you some free time, too; my Miss Jenkins will look after all of them.'

'And in return they must come to us.'

'I'll take it as settled. I'm sure your sister will agree. It was a delightful evening, please thank her for us. I'll be calling later, when I have disposed of this shopping. Viennese shops are such a temptation, I come home with far more than I go out for, every time.'

'Fanny does too,' Julia said. Her sister was most generous, and insisted on buying Julia new gowns and dancing slippers and numerous pairs of gloves, as well as a smart pelisse and several hats.

'I can't have my sister going about in rags,' she'd declared.

'What does Frederick say to your spending all this money on me?'

'He doesn't know. He may appear mean in some ways, but he doesn't scrutinize my dressmaker's bills,' Fanny said. 'He wants me to look a credit to him. And he'd soon complain if he felt you were letting him down.'

★   ★   ★

That, thought Julia, was about the only thing Frederick did not complain about. After two nights when he didn't come back to the apartment, he had reappeared without a word of explanation, and proceeded to find fault with everything from the food that was provided to the quality of the writing paper in the bureau.

'But Frederick, you bought that yourself,' Fanny was unwise enough to point out.

'I can't have done, I wouldn't have bought such rubbish. You and Julia must have used up what I bought with your endless letter writing, or given it to the girls to scribble on, and replaced it, thinking I would not notice.'

Fanny cast up her eyes. 'Believe what you will,' she snapped, to Julia's astonishment. She had never before heard her sister answer Frederick in such a fashion. Perhaps Fanny was at long last beginning to assert herself. Inwardly Julia cheered. It was about time.

Next it was the gowns they were to wear to the Metternich ball exercising Frederick's attention.

53

'The ladies will all be wearing blue and silver,' he stated at breakfast.

'How boring,' Julia said, and laughed. Fanny had insisted on buying her a very pretty rose-coloured gown, and she was planning to wear that.

'You were not asked your opinion,' he retorted. 'I cannot have my family look out of place. If you don't have the right gowns go out today and buy them.'

So she was his family now, was she? Julia was not sure she wanted to be counted as such.

'The ball is tomorrow!' Fanny said. 'If it's as you say and all the ladies mean to wear those colours the shops must have run out of the material days ago. We'd have to buy gowns already made up, and there's no time for alterations.'

'You'll manage, if you want to go. And you'll need olive wreaths in your hair. It's a Peace Ball — have you forgotten? — to celebrate the victory at Leipzig a year ago.'

He rose from the table and left the room, and Julia could contain her splutter of laughter no longer. 'Olive wreaths,' she said.

'Laurel wreaths are very fashionable in London,' Fanny said, 'though I have never liked them.'

'It's a wonder we are not all expected to

wear the sword of victory, but I expect that would get in the way of the dancing.'

'How on earth are we to obtain blue or silver dresses?' Fanny demanded. 'I have that blue morning dress, but it's not suitable for a ball!'

'The girls are going to play with the Pryce children this morning, so I'll go out straight away and see what I can find. We both have white gowns, and if we made military style sashes of blue and silver perhaps that would do. I cannot imagine every single lady will be wearing the same colours. Heavens, there are almost two thousand people attending! A thousand olive wreaths,' she said, laughing again. 'Unless the men are wearing them too. But I doubt any but the Prince Regent would agree to look so ridiculous.'

'Hush!' Fanny said automatically. She was always uncomfortable when anyone said disparaging things about the Prince, though Julia knew she despised him and his Carlton House Set.

'Do you think there are any olive trees in the Prater or the Augarten that we can rob, or don't they grow here? And I promised to take the girls to see the Victory Parade there this afternoon.'

'If you can find some material, I can do the sewing. We mustn't disappoint them.'

Julia nodded. They were going with the Pryce girls and their governess, Miss Jenkins, and at the suggestion of Mrs Pryce, they had brought a picnic.

'I'm told there will be twenty thousand veterans,' Mr Pryce told her. 'It will take hours for them all to pass. But I suppose it's an historic occasion, and the children ought to see it.'

The younger girls were most interested in the colourful uniforms. It meant nothing to them that these men had fought in one of the recent battles against Napoleon, at Leipzig, one which had been a great victory for the Allies, and when Napoleon's last ally, Saxony, had deserted him. All they knew of the defeated Emperor was the threat often used by nursery maids, that if they did not behave well 'Boney' would come and spirit them away.

★　★　★

Frederick smirked as he handed Fanny into the carriage that was to take them to the Metternich mansion in the Rennweg. 'I knew you would find a way if I insisted,' he said.

'It was Julia's idea. She found the silver gauze shawls and I made them into overskirts, and cut up my blue dress for the sashes.'

Julia touched the tiny spray of olive leaves which had been all she'd been able to find, which she had fixed into her hair. It was a wonder Frederick had not objected to the lack of proper wreaths. But he was looking excited, and she wondered whether he was expecting to meet his Russian *inamorata* there.

There was a long line of carriages waiting to set the guests down at the entrance to Prince Metternich's summer palace a short distance outside the city ramparts, and Julia was able to admire the long low lines of it, and the classical porticoes. It was half an hour before Fanny and her party were able to pass up the long flight of red-carpeted stairs to the ballroom, in a specially built pavilion, also pillared in the Classical style.

Frederick disappeared, to Julia's disgust, but Fanny's hand was soon solicited for the polonaise. Julia wandered through one of the many archways into the garden. It was still amazingly warm for the middle of October, and she didn't need a wrap. Hearing the faint sound of an orchestra she walked on through the garden, passing a temple to Apollo, partly hidden by the profuse greenery, and came eventually to a small alcove where the musicians were playing.

She found a stone bench and sat down to

listen. For several days now she had scarcely ever been alone. During the daytime, if she were not teaching the children or taking them for walks in the Viennese parks, she was with Fanny, trying to keep up her sister's spirits. Or she was searching the shops for silver gauze, she recalled, and glanced down at her own over-skirt. It really didn't look like a last minute, cobbled together affair. Frederick had passed no disparaging remarks, so it must be satisfactory.

Was Frederick's behaviour, his pursuit of other women, normal with married men? Until now she had believed that Fanny did not care, but her sister clearly still loved her unsatisfactory husband, and was desperately hurt by his neglect. She ought to set up her own flirt, Julia thought, angry for her sister, and for all the other women who were treated so disdainfully by their menfolk.

She would never endure such humiliation. The thought, unaccountably, brought to mind Sir Carey Evelegh, and she tried, without success, to dismiss him from her thoughts. It was useless for her to even think of marriage, and he was already spoken for. Even if she had ever had the slightest chance of attracting his attention, her lack of fortune would have made her ineligible. She sighed. It would have to be a life as a governess or companion, and her best hope of ever marrying was that a desperate curate, as impecunious as herself, would be in need of a wife to help him in his parish duties.

Julia didn't want to be a wife valued only for her good works, she told herself. Wealthy, landed people married for practical reasons, to consolidate estates, or gain influence, or provide heirs for their lands and titles. Poor people, the peasants she had known in her father's parish, married for other reasons, but whether these were for lust or love, or necessity, she didn't know. She grinned. It had always puzzled her, when she was of an age to know a little about the process of pregnancy and childbirth, how many premature births had occurred in the parish. Then, mulling over one of her father's most vehement sermons, she had understood.

She was in that uncomfortable middle section of society. She had no chance of marrying for the usual reasons of status and money, and it would be frowned upon if she chose her husband from the merchant or peasant classes.

The musicians finished the collection of sonatas they had been playing, and began to wrap up their instruments. Julia suspected they were going to find some food, and the thought made her hungry. Rising, she made her way back to the main pavilion, pausing only to watch one of the *tableaux vivants*. There were several of these, and she promised herself she would look for more, and perhaps watch one of the ballets, when she had satisfied her hunger.

As she approached the buffet she heard her name called, and swinging round saw Sir Carey bearing down on her.

'I wondered where you were,' he said. 'I saw your sister, but it's such a crush I despaired of ever finding you. What do you think of it all?'

Julia's heart was racing at the idea that he had looked for her especially, and then she told herself not to be foolish. It was just the sort of flattering remark any man might make, without meaning it. And he was engaged to be married, and from his description of Angelica, very much in love with her.

'Let's go and find a table,' he said now. 'Then when we have eaten will you honour me with a waltz? I believe there are to be some Russian dances, but despite my time there I never managed to perform them to my satisfaction.'

'Is the conga a Russian dance?' Julia asked when they had helped themselves to platefuls of food. 'I didn't see it, but I understand the

60

Tsar led one through the Hofburg at the masked ball.'

He laughed. 'No, it's not Russian, though their dances are often as boisterous. But Alexander is excelling himself for rudeness tonight,' he added. 'He's telling everyone who will listen how much he prefers the company of soldiers. If the Congress fails, it will be largely his fault. But enough of political matters. How is little Paula? Not fretting about her singing, is she?'

'She seems happy enough, though she has refused to learn the new song I found for them. It will take some time for her to forget what happened.'

How thoughtful of him to ask, she was thinking. Most men would have forgotten the incident, and not been at all concerned about the feelings of a child.

They danced two waltzes, and then, seeing Fanny standing at the side of the ballroom, made their way to her.

'You look pale,' Julia said. 'Are you all right?'

'Of course. It's just so hot in here.'

'Let's walk out in the gardens for a while,' Sir Carey said. 'I believe there is to be a balloon ascent, and fireworks.'

He gave each lady an arm and led them out to where they could sit on another of the

61

benches. Almost immediately there was an explosion of fireworks, which made Fanny jump.

'Look, they are making patterns in the sky,' Julia pointed. 'What are they, do you suppose?'

'That one looks like the British coat of arms,' Sir Carey said. 'And now the Russian. How ingenious.'

After a while Fanny began to shiver, and they went back towards the ballroom. On the way they met Prince Metternich and his wife, who stopped and said a few gracious words.

He was tall and elegant, with blond curly hair. He was, Julia had been told, an excellent horseman and a good swimmer, though she doubted he would be swimming in the River Danube just now. Julia could understand why so many women seemed attracted to him, despite his reputation for being stiff and condescending. His wife Eleonore was small and plain, but she had been possessed of a large dowry, and Metternich's family estates in the Rhineland had been lost during the wars. She seemed gentle, but her smile was wistful and Julia detected a sad expression in her eyes.

Fanny was overcome, commenting as they moved away on how charming they were.

'I don't know how she endures his affairs,'

Sir Carey said. 'He is so blatant over them.'

Julia glanced at him. She felt instinctively that he was not the sort of man either to have affairs, or, if he did, to flaunt them.

He asked Fanny to dance, but she excused herself, saying she was feeling tired and would prefer to sit quietly at the side and watch.

'Shall I go and find Frederick?' Julia asked. Not that he would be of much use, she thought, but at least she might persuade him Fanny ought to go home. It was long after midnight, and she was looking pale and exhausted.

'No, dear, you dance. This is an occasion you will want to remember all your life. You must make the most of it.'

So Julia danced once more with Sir Carey, and then with various other men, mostly Austrian officers who had been present at the victory parade earlier that day in the Prater, and were full of pride at the splendour of the show and the hospitality their city was providing for so many important people.

From time to time Julia went back to Fanny, and was relieved that her sister had been joined by Mrs Pryce and a few of her older friends. They seemed content to sit and gossip, so Julia gave herself up to the pleasure of the occasion. She would never again, she was sure, be involved in such a spectacular party. She'd overheard more than one person saying it put even the Hofburg parties in the shade.

At last, however, Fanny admitted she was tired, and Julia went with her to order the carriage. Frederick was nowhere to be found, and he, she told herself, could walk home. It was what he deserved for his neglect of Fanny. They hadn't seen him all evening.

There was a tremendous crush of departing guests, but eventually Julia found a footman to send for their carriage. These were arriving in an endless line, but Julia could see it would be an hour or more before their own appeared. She glanced round. There were so many people on the huge flight of stairs she wondered it did not give way. Many of the people, wrapped in cloaks, were sitting on the stairs, and she turned to suggest to Fanny that they make their way to the side and do the same.

Fanny was even paler than before, and as Julia caught her arm, she uttered a faint moan and sank to the floor, swooning.

Julia exclaimed in dismay, and bent over her sister.

'Fanny, are you all right? Oh, please, give her room,' she said to the people crowding round her. 'She needs air.'

'Let me.'

It was Sir Carey, who had miraculously appeared beside her. He bent down and with no apparent effort lifted Fanny in his arms. Julia, almost unconsciously, noticed the muscles in his arms and legs as he straightened up. He forced a way through the crowd, uttering apologies, and carried Fanny down the stairs to where there was more space. Julia followed in his wake, clutching the reticule Fanny had dropped, in which she knew there were smelling salts.

At the bottom of the stairs Sir Carey spoke to one of the footmen, and a lady just entering a coach, overhearing, turned towards him.

'Lift your wife in here, sir, and we will convey her to your home. It could be hours before your own carriage can be brought up.'

Fanny was passed, like a parcel, Julia thought rather hysterically, into the coach, and Sir Carey helped her in too, then sprang in himself after giving the coachman the direction. Julia had the smelling salts in her hand, and Fanny soon revived, rather tearful, and bewildered to find herself in a coach with strangers.

They turned out to be a German count and countess from a small duchy north of Bavaria, who brushed aside Julia's thanks.

'What else would anyone do? It was a magnificent occasion, of course, but there were so many lights the ballroom and the entrance were far too hot. It is not surprising the lady swooned.'

By the time they reached their building Fanny was able to walk, and after thanking her rescuers, she was helped by Julia and Sir Carey to climb the stairs to their apartment.

'Sir Carey, you've been so kind.'

'Nonsense. If you will be all right now I'll go back and find Sir Frederick, he must be wondering what has happened to you.'

I doubt that, Julia thought as she and Maggie helped Fanny into bed. Frederick cared only for his own enjoyment. He was more likely to blame Fanny for causing an incident which might have been embarrassing to him.

4

Fanny was unwell for several days, keeping to her room. She confided to Julia that she had overheard Mrs Webber at the Metternich ball speculating about Julia, saying she had heard rumours that Julia had been wise to leave England because of some scandal attached to her.

'What on earth could she have meant?'

Julia laughed. 'You said she was an incorrigible gossip. She's also a crony of Frau Gunter, and that old witch threatened I'd be sorry for opposing her. I wonder if there is any connection? How else could Mrs Webber even pretend to know anything about me? We've never met before.'

Fanny seemed satisfied, though annoyed that Frau Gunter could be so vindictive, and Julia dismissed it from her thoughts. She was more concerned about Frederick's behaviour and the misery this was causing her sister.

Frederick had arrived home long past dawn after the Peace Ball, but to Julia's surprise, made no mention of their own journey home. From Frederick's coachman, Evans, she learnt that, on his finally reaching the point for picking up passengers, and finding no one there, he had been moved on by the footmen. Retreating, he had awaited another summons, assuming the first had been a mistake, but when none came, and there were barely a dozen carriages left, he had returned home.

So Frederick had not wanted his carriage, Julia thought. Had he been off again with his Russian mistress? Julia was utterly convinced that the Countess Tania was indeed his mistress, since he spent very few nights at the apartment, and offered no explanations as to where he had been.

She attempted to distract Fanny by talking about the Congress. Mr Pryce seemed to know many of the English delegation, and almost daily he brought Fanny and Julia news of what was happening in the negotiations.

'The Tsar and Metternich had another confrontation,' he said a few days after the Parade. 'You heard how the Tsar insulted him at Metternich's own ball, saying soldiers such as he had to be shot because of the decisions taken by the diplomats?'

'We heard of it afterwards,' Fanny said. 'But what now?'

'Alexander sent for him, and raged at him for two hours, blaming Austria for the Polish question not being settled. He even threatened him with a sword.'

'Not very regal behaviour,' Julia said. 'What happened then?'

'Metternich offered to resign. He is distraught, they tell me. He has not been himself since the affair with the Duchess of Sagan ended. He took that badly. Now most of the German states are blaming him, saying he ignores their claims in favour of a confederation led by Austria and Prussia.'

'So what will happen? Is this Congress going to last for ever?' Fanny asked, sighing. 'We've been here for six weeks or more, and nothing has yet been decided, it seems.'

'The Emperors and King Frederick are to visit Budapest soon. Perhaps, with them safely occupied, the ministers can get down to some detailed negotiation.'

'Let us hope so,' Fanny said. 'I am so weary of living in these cramped conditions, with no notion of when we will be able to go home. If we don't leave soon we will not be at Greystones for Christmas, and then no doubt we'll be kept here for months afterwards if the roads are impassable due to snow.'

'Can you not persuade Sir Frederick to leave?' Mr Pryce asked. 'He has no official position, he does not have to stay.'

Fanny shook her head. 'He has no desire to go home,' she said quietly. 'We will be here for months.'

'Has Prince Metternich cancelled the costume ball he planned?' Julia asked, anxious to change the subject, for she could see that Fanny was on the verge of tears.

'Not as far as I have heard. I doubt he will. He may be exceedingly unpopular, blamed for the failure to agree on Poland, and suffering at the loss of the Duchess, but he's a strong man.'

★ ★ ★

The costume ball went ahead soon after the rulers returned from Budapest. The women were to wear ethnic dress, and Julia was delighted that Fanny's spirits lifted as they pondered on what might be called an ethnic English costume.

'I think I'll go as a milkmaid,' Julia suggested.

'The churns they carry would be a nuisance while you were dancing,' Fanny said, giggling.

'Mm, yes. But what are we best known for?'

'If we were Welsh we could wear red cloaks and those tall pointed hats. That is what they wear, isn't it?'

'I know! The English are known as sailors and soldiers. I'll go as a Jolly Jack Tar and you

70

can be a soldier. It should be easy to borrow suitable clothes. And I've always wanted to wear trousers!'

'Frederick would never permit it.'

Julia bridled. 'He has no control over me, to tell me what I may or may not wear!'

In the end they compromised by going in the simple kind of gowns worn by village girls and maidservants, made of gingham, with plain white aprons and mob caps. When Fanny saw Julia as they were about to set off, she shook her head, scandalized.

'Julia, you are showing your ankles!'

'But Fanny, how am I to go harvesting, or scrubbing the front doorstep, in a gown that touches the floor?'

She refused to do anything about it, threatening to kilt her gown even higher. 'As the village girls at home did when they were working,' she reminded Fanny.

There was no time to insist, as they knew there would be another crush of carriages in the Rennweg, so Fanny gave way.

If anything, this occasion was even more glittering than the Peace Ball. Everyone of importance was present, and there was a great deal of variety in the gowns. Julia gazed with envy at the pretty and colourful costumes from the different countries, and when she asked one Austrian lady about

71

them, was told that every region had its own variation.

Then she heard a few titters and turned to see what was so amusing.

'Isn't that Lady Castlereagh just coming in?' she whispered to Fanny. 'What on earth has she got in her hair?'

'Disgusting,' someone behind her said. 'It's a mockery, disrespectful!'

'It can't be!' Fanny said, shaking her head. 'She wouldn't dare!'

'Dare what?' Julia demanded impatiently.

'It's exactly like the Order of the Garter. But surely Lord Castlereagh would not permit it?'

It seemed he had, judging by other shocked comments Julia heard from the English guests.

'Emily Hobart always was fat and dowdy,' one woman said. 'I never could understand what he saw in her.'

'But they say he's devoted,' another replied.

'Heaven knows why! Did you hear, they employed a special dancing master to give them lessons,' the first tittered. 'I'm longing to see whether the poor fellow managed to make her any more graceful.'

Julia turned and stared at them, and saw it was Mrs Webber, who had been at Fanny's party. She frowned. This sort of sniggering gossip had been rife during her only Season, and she had hated it then. Her refusal to join in with other debutantes, busy tearing to shreds the faces, figures and reputations of those not in their particular circle, had made her unpopular then. They'd called her a prude, and mocked her. She'd been thankful when she'd been able to go back to the country, and had lost no time finding herself a position where she did not have to meet such people.

'Charmingly rustic,' said Sir Carey, coming up to them.

Julia promptly forgot the gossips, and turned to him, smiling. 'Why can't we have a proper English national dress?' she asked. 'Most of the English have not bothered to use their imaginations. Especially the men,' she added, grinning up at him.

'I admit it! Should I have worn a footman's livery? Or come as a chimney sweep or butcher?'

'With dirty clothes? Why, no one would have cared to dance with you! But you must admit men have a wider choice of costume, so I think it ill of you not to have bothered!'

He laughed. 'As I am not dirty, come and dance with me.'

'Is there ever to be any progress?' she asked later, when they were sipping champagne. 'From all we hear the Congress is falling apart.'

'Don't despair. It's always difficult when so many different people all want contradictory things. But we can't afford to fail.'

★ ★ ★

During November and December the negotiations went on. Julia followed the twists and turns with interest, but Fanny was sunk too much in misery to want to know all the intricacies of the different alliances and the quarrels, particularly between the Tsar and Metternich. Frederick spent only half his time at the apartment, and he did not bother to deny that he spent the rest of it with the Countess Tania. Occasionally Fanny roused herself to take some interest in the entertainments Vienna continued to offer the visitors, but she refused more invitations than she accepted, saying she felt too weak to want to face the crowds at balls and receptions. Julia suspected she wanted to avoid Mrs Webber's vicious tongue. Fanny was unable to ignore gossip as she did herself.

Julia regretted not being able to go to the Carrousel, a mock tournament held in the Riding Hall, where the best Austrian riders competed in medieval events, sporting the ladies' favours.

'The cheapest sash cost a thousand

gulden,' Mrs Pryce told her, awed. 'I don't know how everyone is managing, they have to have elaborate new gowns for every occasion.'

Fanny was persuaded to attend the concert where Beethoven, despite his deafness, conducted his own work. As well as the Seventh Symphony he had written a new piece to celebrate the victory at Vittoria.

'Thank goodness there are no more balls,' she said as they were driven home afterwards. 'It will soon be Advent.'

Meanwhile the political negotiations became more and more tense.

'Perhaps if the Tsar were well things would move more swiftly,' Fanny complained. 'They say he is sulking.'

'It cannot go on for ever,' Julia tried to console her.

She was very worried about her sister, convinced Fanny's listlessness came more from her unhappiness about Frederick's behaviour than a physical malaise. Then help came from an unexpected quarter.

★   ★   ★

Sir Carey, being privy to Lord Castlereagh's thoughts, knew better than most how precariously balanced the situation was. The letters he received from friends in England were worrying, too. The government, not really interested in European affairs, was becoming impatient, and there were many disapproving noises about Castlereagh's conduct of the negotiations.

'They should be here, to see what he has to contend with,' he said bitterly one afternoon when he met Julia outside some shops, and persuaded her to have coffee and some *sachertorte* with him at one of the many cafés.

'Is it impossible?' Julia asked.

'A settlement? Sometimes I think so. Both the Tsar and Frederick William are unpredictable men. If they don't get what they want, I fear there could be another war.'

He shouldn't have said that, he thought, seeing how pale Julia went. But she was such an intelligent and attentive listener, he sometimes forgot to be discreet.

'War? Ought I to insist Fanny goes home?'

'I'm being pessimistic. France is on our side now, and though we won't get a strong and united Poland, I'm sure something satisfactory can be worked out.'

When she left he pulled the last letter from Angelica from his pocket and read it again. She was excited to be joining a large house party in Yorkshire for the Christmas season, but unusually, she did not complain that he would not be there with her. He smiled. She seemed more grown up, and had realized it was impossible for him to desert Lord Castlereagh now, so had ceased demanding it of him. He would, however, have to leave Vienna by the end of February. Come what may, he intended to be home in England in plenty of time for their wedding.

★ ★ ★

Frederick reappeared at the apartment a few days before Christmas. An hour later Klara announced Frau Gunter, who stalked in and settled herself in the most comfortable chair before Fanny had a chance to greet her.

Julia tensed. What did the old woman want? She had not bothered much with them for weeks now.

'Has that renegade husband of yours arrived?' she demanded.

'Frederick?' Fanny stammered.

'How many husbands do you have, ninny?'

'He — he has just now come in.'

'Good. Make sure you keep him here this time. That hussy has been sent away, and I expect Frederick to behave himself now. I've told him he'll see none of my money when I'm gone if he doesn't stop this ridiculous philandering. I'd send you home to England if it weren't likely to snow and block the roads. Well, what do you say?'

Fanny cast a terrified look at Julia, who was having difficulty suppressing her thoughts as she imagined the confrontation there must have been between this old harridan and Frederick. He would have stammered like a schoolboy, and the threat of being cut out of her will would have brought him to heel.

'I — thank you,' Fanny managed, and Frau Gunter seemed content.

She rose to her feet. 'You are to inform me at once if he spends a night away from home, or you discover him going to her at any time. I have my own methods of knowing where she is, and if she dares to return to Vienna. In such a case I will expect to see Frederick at once, so that I can make sure he understands I am quite resolved. Good morning.'

Julia and Fanny were too astonished to do more than stare after her as she swept out of the room. The front door slammed, and Julia let out a peal of laughter.

'Well, what do you make of that?'

There was a hopeful look in Fanny's eyes. 'Do you think he'll obey her?' she asked hesitantly.

'Time will tell. I wonder what he'll be like?'

'Angry, no doubt. But if he stays here I know I can make him forget her!' Fanny said, and smiled for what seemed the first time in weeks.

Julia wondered. Frederick might have been cowed for now by his formidable grandmother, but how long would it last? Even if the Countess Tania had been banished — and how in the world had Frau Gunter contrived that? — there were plenty of other women in Vienna looking for the excitement of an illicit liaison.

★　★　★

Frau Gunter's power was greater than Julia had imagined, she admitted to herself a few days later. Frederick did his best to appear pleasant, and even took the girls to see the Christmas tree one of the bankers had imported, the first, he said, to be seen in Vienna.

Christmas was happy for Fanny and the girls, and Julia rejoiced to see this harmony. She didn't want to hazard a guess as to how long it would last, but allowed herself to enjoy the peace.

Fanny was blooming again, with colour in her cheeks and brightness in her eyes. Even the news that the Russian Embassy, full of wonderful treasures, had burnt down and been completely destroyed on the last day of the year did not dim her happiness.

'It had been given by a wealthy Russian Count, and they regularly had suppers there for over three hundred people,' Mrs Pryce told them. 'It even had a heating system, something like the Romans used to have during their empire,' she added. 'I don't have any idea how it worked, but Mr Pryce could tell you. He's fascinated by all these new scientific machines.'

In January there was snow, which delighted the girls, especially when Sir Carey took them on a sleigh ride into the Wienerwald. The Polish question had, he told Julia, been finally settled.

'But Lord Castlereagh is to go home, he is needed to defend the settlement in Parliament.'

'Then who will negotiate for us here?'

He smiled. 'The Duke himself.'

'Wellington?' Julia gasped.

'The very one. His reputation is such I feel confident he can get them all to agree on the remaining matters.'

'Will you be going home with Lord Castlereagh?' Julia asked, suddenly aware that their time here might be coming to an end.

'I promised Angelica I would be home for our wedding in spring, and I can hardly miss that. I will probably be travelling with

Castlereagh, but he won't be going until the Duke arrives and they have had a chance to confer.'

And I will not see you again, Julia thought to herself. She'd known they would one day part, and she had no cause to complain. She wondered when Frederick would decide he'd had enough of Vienna and set off home. Not until the snow had gone, she suspected. Then she would have to begin looking for another position herself.

★ ★ ★

The Duke arrived at the beginning of February, and Sir Frederick departed.

Julia came in one day with the girls, all of them rosy-cheeked from having been playing in the snow, to find Fanny in floods of tears, and Maggie desperate.

'I can't get her to stop, miss,' Maggie gasped. 'I found her like this when I came back from marketing. She won't tell me what's the matter, but she'll make herself ill if she goes on like this.'

'There must be some smelling salts in her room. Fetch me those, and then take the children away and keep them amused. Don't look so frightened, Alice. Your mama will soon be better. Be a good girl and play with

Paula until I come to you.'

Maggie took the children away, and Julia sat beside Fanny and took her hand.

'Fanny, dear, what is the matter? Are you ill? Have you had bad news? Tell me what it is, and we can share it.'

Fanny gulped and handed Julia a crumpled sheet of paper. As Maggie came back with the smelling salts at that moment she left the paper while persuading Fanny to sit up properly and try to be calm. When Fanny's sobs had dwindled into the occasional hiccup Julia spread out the sheet of paper, smoothing it down on her knee.

It was short and to the point.

I find I cannot endure life without Tania. We have gone away together to her home. When the roads are in better condition, hire another coach and go back to England. I will arrange matters with my man of business soon. I have left a roll of money in your dressing case. It should be enough for your needs until you are home and can call on my bankers.

5

Fanny refused to leave Vienna.

'He will come back,' she protested, when Julia tried to persuade her to follow Frederick's orders to go home. 'I know he will, and if I'm not here for him, he may go back to — to her!'

'He's gone to Russia with her,' Julia said patiently. 'Even if he turns back soon, it could be several days. And he might choose not to come back here. He'll be too ashamed to face people, I'd imagine. Besides, he'll expect you to have set off back home, so he is more likely to head there.'

'He will come back,' Fanny insisted. 'I have to wait here for him, or he will not know where to find me.'

She was oblivious to the excitement attending the Duke's arrival. However, as he caught a cold and remained for some days in Castlereagh's rooms, the people gradually lost their interest in him. The crowds waiting to catch a glimpse of the military hero grew less, as people went about their own business. They would no doubt have plenty of time to see him later.

Frau Gunter, denied entry on the grounds that Fanny was too ill to see anyone, waylaid Julia and the children one day when they were coming back from a visit to the market.

'Tell your sister I have lost all patience with her,' she hissed. 'I get rid of that Russian trollop and bring her husband back to her, at no little inconvenience for myself, and she's not clever enough to keep him. I wash my hands of her and all her family.'

'And of your grandson?' Julia asked, her voice as cold as the slush on the road. 'Surely his is the main fault? He did not have to make such a cake of himself by running off with the wretched woman.'

Frau Gunter glared at her. 'I didn't ask for your opinion. No man will stray if his wife satisfies him, and looks after his needs.'

Julia snorted inelegantly. 'Where have you lived? Are you blind? Can you not see unfaithful husbands all around you here in Vienna? Is every wife inadequate? Can you honestly say your husband never strayed?' And if I'd been her husband I'd have been off like a shot, she added to herself.

'You're an impertinent chit, not fit to be in charge of my great-grandchildren. Heaven knows what you are teaching them!'

'I thought you had disowned them?' Julia asked sweetly. 'In which case you can have no possible interest in what I teach them. Goodbye, Frau Gunter.' I hope your spleen chokes you, she added under her breath.

Julia renewed her efforts to persuade Fanny to leave Vienna, for everything she saw or heard reminded her of Frederick, and she was constantly in tears. Then fate took a hand.

They received a message from Frau Schwartz that the Congress was going on for too long, so she was returning and wished to reclaim the apartment in four days, and trusted they would not be too inconvenienced, as they could always return to stay with Frau Gunter.

★ ★ ★

In between his semi-official duties Sir Carey found time to worry about not hearing from Angelica. However often he told himself that she was at best an indifferent correspondent, and during the Christmas festivities would have had less time than usual, he grew more and more concerned. Was she ill? Had some accident befallen her? Was she snowbound on the Yorkshire moors, at her house party?

Of course letters were lost. Some people, to make sure their news was delivered, might send two letters in the hope one would get through. But Angelica did not do that. He almost laughed at the thought of her penning two copies of her short letters.

He found time to visit Lady Cunningham, but Julia said she was too distraught to see anyone. No wonder, he thought, for all Vienna knew of Sir Frederick's elopement.

'Give her my regards, if you will, and remember, if there is anything I can do, call on me.'

'Are you busy?'

'Moderately. Lord Castlereagh and the Duke need to spend a great deal of time together, there is so much to report, and the twists and turns of the negotiations all need to be explained. But with the question of Poland out of the way, even if we did not succeed in reuniting the country, the rest of the settlements should not take too much time. Many have already been almost agreed.'

Julia nodded. 'I shall always be grateful to have been here, and seen history being made,' she said.

'Despite what has happened to your sister?' he asked gently. It had not been a happy time for Lady Cunningham, and she seemed to be totally dependent on Julia for support. That must have been a strain on her, but she seemed a capable enough young woman.

'I think it would have happened one day, wherever we were. Frederick always had an

86

eye for a pretty woman, and he's a restless sort of person. He'd have left Fanny in the end, I feel sure. I just wish she didn't love him so. Love can be a trap.'

'You will not think so when you fall in love,' he said, and smiled as he thought of his own dear love. 'Is there no fortunate man waiting for you in England?'

Julia smiled ruefully. 'Who, apart from a poor curate, would want to marry a portionless girl, especially now, when scandal has engulfed her family?'

He found nothing to say to this. She spoke the truth. Marriage without a dowry was unlikely. Pretty as she was, most men regarded marriage as a business arrangement, and if they liked the girl they married, that was a bonus. He doubted if many couples shared the sort of devotion he and Angelica enjoyed. Now Fanny's troubles would affect Julia. If she did attract the attention of some poor curate, the scandal attached to Fanny's husband would deter him. It seemed as though she would have to settle for a life as a companion or governess. A pity, with her looks and intelligence. She would have been an admirable helpmeet for a bishop, let alone a curate.

He soon took his leave, and went back to fretting about the lack of letters from

Angelica. Some time ago he had written to ask her whether she wished to make an extended round of visits to their relations, and if so, where did hers live, so that he could make plans.

He told himself he would hear soon, and forced himself to concentrate on the work he was doing for Lord Castlereagh.

* * *

I'll never see him again, Julia thought as she watched him walk away. Then she turned to more pressing concerns. Somehow she had to force Fanny to face reality, and set off on the long journey to England. They had three days in which to make plans.

In desperation Fanny had suggested asking Frau Gunter to shelter them, but Julia poured scorn on the idea.

'She would not speak to us, let alone share her apartment with us,' Julia insisted. 'Let me make arrangements, Fanny, before we run through all the money Frederick left you. It wasn't a generous amount.'

Fanny shook her head. 'Let us wait one more day. He might come back. He left her once. It must be just infatuation.'

Frustrated, Julia went to fetch the girls, who were spending more time with the Pryce children while she was needed to keep Fanny company.

'She won't agree to go,' she said to Mrs Pryce. 'Nothing I say will persuade her to make the effort to arrange the journey. I truly believe she imagines we can remain in this apartment.'

'Well, Mr Pryce and I have been thinking. He must go back soon, for Lord Castlereagh will need his support in Parliament. So would Fanny come with us?'

Julia looked at her, hope in her eyes. 'She might,' she said. 'That's very kind of you. I'll talk her into it, if I have to talk for days and nights on end till she is exhausted.'

'Then let us think about the practicalities. There are seven of us, with my maid and Mr Pryce's valet. The coach will hold eight, but no more in comfort. Though the children are small, they take less room. What I suggest is that Edward's valet, Spicer, travels in the second coach, with the luggage, and if you did not mind, you and Maggie could travel with him. Miss Jenkins will help to keep Fanny's daughters amused, and my maid, Bessie, can help Fanny. I can't do without either of them. Mr Pryce may have to do without his valet for a while,' she added, and laughed.

'But won't the coaches travel together?'

Julia asked. 'We only brought one; there was room for the luggage as well as us, so I don't know how it is arranged.'

'We will try to keep together, but it isn't always possible. With your and Fanny's luggage as well as ours and, if Fanny is like me, there will be far more going back than we brought with us, that coach may be too laden to keep up. We cannot afford to delay if we are to reach London in good time. Don't worry, Williams is a very reliable coachman, and Spicer is totally trustworthy. He will have funds to pay your shot at the inns. What do you say?'

'It sounds an ideal solution,' Julia said slowly. 'All we have to do is persuade Fanny. Will you come back with me and add your arguments to mine?'

★ ★ ★

To Julia's relief, Fanny raised few objections, which the energetic Mrs Pryce soon disposed of. An hour later she departed to make arrangements, and inform her spouse he would in all likelihood have to manage without his valet for much of the three weeks or more it took to reach London.

Julia and Maggie set about packing, The children, who had been subdued since their

90

father had left, became very excited when told they were going home, and travelling with their friends Amelia and Charlotte. They did not understand, until the two coaches were at the door, that Julia would not be travelling in theirs.

Paula began to cry. 'I want to go with Aunt Julia,' she sobbed, clinging to Julia's hand.

'I'll be right behind you,' Julia said, lifting her into the coach. 'You can wave to me out of the window. And we will be together every time we stop for food, or to sleep.'

Time enough, she thought, for Paula to discover they might not be able to keep up with the lighter, faster coach. Luckily Fanny had divided the money Frederick had left her and given half to Julia.

'We don't want to be beholden to Edward Pryce,' she said, 'so you can pay for your and Maggie's accommodation, and if we are separated you have money for emergencies.'

'I have most of what you have given me as salary,' Julia protested. 'Why should you pay more?'

'I brought you here; it's my responsibility.'

There had been no opportunity to say farewell to Sir Carey, and in one way Julia was thankful. Seeing him would only reawaken silly longings. She had effectively made the break the last time they had met.

As they drove out of Vienna she looked back for the last time at the magnificent buildings. It had been a magical time, an experience she would never forget, something she could never have dreamed of a few months ago.

There was still snow on the ground, but on the roads it had been beaten down, and the horses had no difficulty keeping their feet. They were to go by way of Linz and Passau, then across Germany and through the Low Countries. It was over 700 miles to the coast, and then there would be the crossing, and the final journey to London.

Elizabeth Pryce had promised, if they were separated, as seemed likely, to keep Fanny with her in London until Julia could rejoin them there. She would deal with what happened then, whether Fanny would want to go to Greystones at once, or remain in London. There was little point in fretting. Or in worrying about what Frederick would do. Would he try to divorce Fanny? Was he so infatuated with his wretched Countess Tania that he might wish to marry her? If he did, Fanny would need to be provided for, and Julia could foresee endless problems, as well as more heartache for her sister.

She settled down to enjoy the wintry landscape, the river valleys they followed, the snow-covered trees on the hillsides, and the pretty villages they passed through.

After they passed Linz, the coaches drew apart. On the next night Julia's party halted at a large inn as darkness fell, to discover that the first coach had passed through two hours before.

'So we're on our own from now,' Spicer said. 'I must say it's pleasant not to have to start work the moment we reach an inn, washing linen, ironing coats and starching cravats.'

Maggie giggled, and looked apologetically at Julia. 'Like a holiday,' she said. 'Of course, Miss Julia, I'll be helping you.'

'I'm accustomed to looking after myself, Maggie. You have a holiday too.'

★　★　★

Maggie and Spicer had initially been wary of Julia, but she soon put them at their ease, and they chatted together about the country they passed through, and their impressions of Vienna. Julia was amused to discover they knew almost as much as she did about the negotiations, and the disputes which had arisen among the participants.

'Did you know they put lots of people as spies?' Maggie asked, giggling. 'One of the maids at Lord Castlereagh's house told me these servants, the spies, were supposed to go through all the waste-paper baskets every day, and send anything they found which might be interesting to the chief man. Hager, I think his name was.'

'If they knew this, what did they do?' Julia asked.

'Oh, someone had to stay up late burning everything.' She giggled again. 'It's a good job we didn't have need for extra servants.'

'But we had nothing to hide,' Julia pointed out, and shivered. The notion of being spied on in such a way disturbed her. Did the Austrians know in advance what the other ministers were planning? Was it always like this when different countries were trying to make treaties? If Lord Castlereagh's people went to the trouble to burn their papers, presumably it was.

They passed through Passau, and a week after they left Vienna were approaching Nuremberg. Though cold, it was a bright, sunny day, and Spicer had decided he would prefer to ride on the box with Williams. No doubt he found Maggie's chat tedious, and wanted to be away from it. Maggie usually found plenty to chat about. If it wasn't the scenery, or the weather, she would talk about Vienna. Occasionally she mentioned Sir

Frederick, saying how terrible his behaviour was, then she would look apologetically at Julia and change the subject.

'I'm sorry, miss,' she said the first time it happened. 'I forget you're my mistress's sister.'

Julia reassured her, saying she deplored his behaviour too, but she hoped he would remember his duty and return to his family soon, so it was best not to talk about it. She did not want Maggie to become so partisan in defence of Fanny that she risked upsetting Frederick, and she had soon discovered Maggie found it difficult to conceal her feelings. She might remain silent, but she had a very expressive face, and from the way she had glared at one of the pot boys who spilt ale on her gown, Julia could imagine how she would look at Frederick.

★ ★ ★

Lord Castlereagh had finished giving the Duke what information he had, and in mid-February was preparing to set out for England. Sir Carey, who had hoped to travel with him and be reunited at last with Angelica, was disappointed to be asked to stay on for a while, since his knowledge of what had been happening, though unofficial, could prove valuable. He supposed it was true, in that people might talk more freely to him as he was not part of the official delegation.

It was some time since he had seen any of Lady Cunningham's party, and he wondered whether they were also suffering from colds. As he was passing their apartment on his way home one morning he decided to call.

Klara opened the door and smiled at him, but did not invite him to step inside, as she usually did, for she knew he was always a welcome visitor.

'Is Lady Cunningham in?' he asked, and Klara shook her head.

'They left,' she said. 'My mistress is back home.'

'Left? You mean they have moved to another apartment?'

'Oh, no, they have gone to England. With Herr Pryce and his family.'

'All of them?' he asked blankly, and then chastised himself as a fool. Of course they would all have gone. What did he expect?

'Yes, all of them,' Klara said cheerfully, and began to shut the door.

'Did they leave a message?' he asked, and she smiled and shook her head as the door finally closed.

He stared at it, then turned away. Of course

they would not leave him a message. He was just one of many acquaintances. Perhaps they had left in haste, and would not have had time. He would have liked to say farewell. It was unlikely they would meet in England, but he felt a nagging curiosity to learn what happened, whether Sir Frederick tired of his Russian mistress, and whether Lady Cunningham forgave him and took him back.

What would Julia do? She was good with children, and he could imagine her as a governess far better than he could as a companion to some crotchety old lady.

He went on to his own rooms, to find a letter from Angelica waiting for him. He slit it open eagerly. It had been several weeks since he had heard from her, and he was anxious to hear how she was.

* * *

It was almost dusk, and they were passing through a pretty village, planning to stop soon for the night at a large inn a few miles ahead.

'We stayed there on the way here,' Spicer informed Julia.

Maggie was exclaiming at the brightly painted cottages, and the snow which still covered the ground, when the coach tilted alarmingly. Julia looked out of the window and saw they were about to descend a steep slope towards a ford at the bottom of a little river valley.

She hung out of the window, watching anxiously. It was bitterly cold, and she was thankful for her warm cloak with the hood. The slush they had been driving through was hardening into icy ruts. One of the horses slipped, but managed to regain his feet. The coach slowed to a crawl, and they reached the bottom of the slope without mishap. On the opposite side of the river the road rose more gently, and Julia breathed a sigh of relief. If it had been equally as steep the horses might not have been able to pull the coach up it.

She glanced down at the water, very shallow here in the path of the ford, but immediately downstream it seemed to dive into a deep pool, where it swirled and eddied round huge boulders.

They had almost reached the far side, and the horses were out of the water, when Julia heard an ominous cracking sound, and before she could think what it was the coach listed sideways, only prevented from toppling over by one huge boulder.

Maggie fell against Julia, and the door swung open. Because Julia was holding on to it she managed to break her fall, and cling on to the side of the coach, but Maggie, screaming, fell past her, and vanished into the swirling waters of the downstream pool. Julia could not have described exactly what happened next. She was only aware of the luggage, torn from the roof of the coach, falling past her, and being hit by the odd corner as the trunks slithered into the river.

In the midst of the confusion she thought she heard Williams shouting, and then the coach was being dragged along by the terrified horses. She clung on to the wildly swinging door, but it was being torn away from the hinges. Julia glanced desperately over her shoulder, and saw that within moments she would be smashed to pieces against the boulder.

There was only one thing to do, and Julia, taking a deep breath, let go and dropped into the icy water.

6

They were almost at Frankfurt when Fanny accepted the truth. For some days she had tried to persuade herself that the constant nausea she was suffering was no more than the result of the indifferent food they often had at the inns, combined with the jolting of the coach. But she had been pregnant too often to mistake the signs now. Her brief reconciliation with Frederick had been fruitful.

She didn't know whether to be pleased or otherwise. Several times in the past she had conceived, only to lose the child a month or so later. Would it happen again, and if so, would she be relieved or sorry? She loved her children and would have liked a large family. But if she carried this one to term, bringing up another child when the future was so uncertain, and she didn't know whether Frederick would ever return to her, was a daunting prospect. On the other hand, it might prove to be the longed-for son and heir. If that happened, would Frederick come back? If he did, how would she treat him?

Could she ever forgive him for the

100

humiliation he had piled upon her, the unhappiness he had caused? Could she ever trust him not to do it again?

Elizabeth Pryce noticed her abstraction.

'You look pale, my dear,' she said as they prepared to enter the coach one morning. 'Are you suffering from the crowding, or the jolting?'

'Neither,' Fanny reassured her, and decided she had best confide in the woman who had been so kind to her. 'It's just that I am probably breeding.'

Elizabeth looked startled for a moment, then smiled uncertainly. 'Your husband was with you at Christmas?'

'Oh yes, long enough to give me another child. I have lost half a dozen in the past, I don't seem able to carry them to term. So the chances of this one surviving are not good.'

'We must do our best. We've made good time, despite the weather and the state of the roads. We must make sure there is not too much jolting, and we'll stop early so that you don't get too tired. What a shame your sister is not with you. They can't be many days behind, so she'll soon be with you once we reach London.'

* * *

101

Julia awoke to find a smooth-cheeked, bright-eyed face surrounded by a huge white poke bonnet leaning over her. She blinked. No, it wasn't a bonnet. It was the sort of head-dress nuns wore. She'd seen some — where had she seen some recently?

'Good, you have returned to us, by the grace of God,' the woman said in guttural French. 'Do you speak French, child?'

Julia frowned. She understood what was being said, so she must. She nodded.

'Thank goodness. Neither of your companions appears to understand either French or German, and none of us speak English. I believe you are English?'

Julia nodded again. 'What happened?' she tried.

'You do not recall? The coach in which you were travelling had an accident. You were all thrown into the river.'

Suddenly the memory of it came back to Julia in a tumultuous rush. She could remember the dreadful freezing cold of the water, and being swept along as though she were no bigger than a leaf. She shivered, although she did not feel cold now. She could have died, and Fanny would never have known what became of her.

She looked at her surroundings. She was lying in a bed inside what must be a convent cell, for the only other furniture was a small prie-dieu and a crucifix hung on the wall above it. Light seeped through a small window high up on the wall, and Julia vaguely recalled her mother telling her that convent windows were placed high up so that the view did not distract the inmates.

How sad, she'd thought then, not to be able to see the flowers and the trees and all the other wonderful sights of the world, the views limited to the sky and the clouds. And, presumably, the moon and the stars at night, for there were no curtains or shutters she could see.

'How did we get here? Where is Maggie? Is she all right? And the men?'

'They are your family, perhaps?'

Julia shook her head. 'Maggie is my sister's maid. The men are the coachman and valet who work for some friends. We were travelling home — to England — with the luggage because there wasn't room for all of us in the main coach. We had to travel more slowly, so we are a few days behind them. They won't know what's happened to us.'

'You can send a letter to London, it will reach your sister a few days after she arrives at home.'

'Thank you, yes, I'll do that.'

'I see. You will be able to see Maggie

tomorrow. But now I have a drink for you. I expect you are thirsty.'

She helped Julia to sit up and drink. It was pleasant, some sort of fruit tisane, Julia thought, but soon she was too drowsy to ask more questions, and sank back to sleep.

It was dark when she woke again, but there was a lamp, turned low, on the floor in a corner of the room, and a nun sat quietly on a stool beside the bed, telling her beads. When Julia stirred she rose and put a cool palm on Julia's forehead.

'Good, you do not have the fever now.'

'I'm quite well. What time is it? May I get up? Where are my clothes, please? And where is Maggie?'

'So many questions! It's almost dawn. Maggie is being well looked after. I will fetch you some food, and afterwards you may dress and go to see her.'

She would say no more until Julia had eaten some soft, delicious rolls spread with sweet butter and cherry conserve, and drunk a cup of strong, aromatic coffee. She left the room taking the tray with her, and returned with the clothes Julia had been wearing. A second nun followed with a jug of water and some towels, and Julia saw there was a small washstand in the far corner of the cell.

'I will come back for you in a few minutes,'

104

she said. 'I have brought a brush for your hair.'

To her annoyance, Julia felt astonishingly weak. She discovered she was wearing a voluminous nightgown, not her own, and she must have been bathed while she was asleep or unconscious, for her body smelled of delicate flowers, not rank river water, and she could smell the same on the soap which rested on the towels. She managed to strip off the nightgown and wash, then she struggled into her own clothes, which were freshly laundered, the underclothes smelling of lavender. Her woollen gown had, she saw, been expertly washed, but it had shrunk a little from its immersion in the river, and clung to her body. Some of the dye had been lost, but it was warm and she was thankful to have it. In addition there was a thick shawl, which she pulled round her shoulders.

She brushed her hair, which had also been washed. How long had she been unconscious, and how deeply, for her to be treated like that and not be aware of it?

Instead of her own boots there was a pair of soft leather slippers, lined with fur, and thankfully she slipped them on. The room was cold. Then she sank down on to the bed, feeling unaccountably weak after the effort.

A minute or so later the nun returned.

'Are you able to walk?' she asked.

'I feel weak,' Julia confessed, 'but I must see Maggie.'

'First the Mother Superior wishes to talk to you. She is anxious to know who you are and where you were going, so that she can send messages to your friends who may be expecting you, and worrying. You can include a note for them.'

★ ★ ★

Julia felt amazingly unsteady as she was led along a series of wide passageways and into a bare room containing no more than a plain table and a few chairs. A tall, distinguished-looking nun, who was standing beside the window, turned and came towards her, smiling.

'I am pleased to see you looking better,' she said. 'Please, sit down, and tell me about yourselves.'

Julia explained quickly. 'The last thing I remember is Maggie falling into the pool beside the ford, and then I jumped into the water because the horses were dragging the coach and I was afraid it would fall over and I would be crushed. Is Maggie here? How is she? And how long have we been here?'

'It's three days since the accident. I am told

a wheel came off the carriage. You were unconscious for a while, and had a fever, but fortunately you don't appear to have harmed your head or your body. The villagers pulled you out and brought you here.'

'Three days!'

The Mother Superior smiled. 'Indeed. Unfortunately the villagers did not bring any of your belongings, so we had nothing to tell us who you were. They swore everything had been washed away,' she added dryly. 'Washed into their cottages, I suspect.'

Julia knew there were things here she needed to worry about, but she was more concerned with Maggie, and once more asked after her.

'Sister Maria tells me she is your sister's maid. She will get better, I assure you, but she seemed to have been in the water much longer than you were, and she has been very ill. We are praying it will not turn to consumption, but she will be unfit to travel for several weeks. You may go and see her in a few minutes.'

'And the men? The coachman and Mr Pryce's valet?'

'Is that who they are? The older man, he is the coachman?'

'Yes, Spicer is quite young.'

'Poor man! The coachman apparently got

his legs entangled in the reins as he fell, and he suffered a broken leg. It is, the doctor tells me, mending well, but he will not be fit to travel for some weeks either. He is being looked after by the monks at their abbey a few miles away.'

'And Spicer?'

The nun crossed herself. 'He struck his head on one of the boulders when he fell, and I'm sorry to tell you he broke his neck. We have said masses for his soul, and he will be buried in the village churchyard as soon as the ground is soft enough for a grave to be dug.'

★　★　★

Maggie was lucid, for almost the first time since she had been brought to the convent, Sister Maria told Julia. She was also tearful, and fretting about what Lady Cunningham would do without her.

'How soon can we go home, miss?' she asked.

'I don't know, Maggie,' Julia said, 'but my sister will not blame you, and you will not lose your job. Besides, you are not well enough to travel yet.'

And how, Julia wondered, when she was back in her own room and lying down on the bed to recover from her exertions, were they to get back to England? She thought of the young valet, being killed in such a fashion. He had been cheerful company, and she shed a few tears for him.

'Were all our possessions lost?' she asked Sister Maria when the latter brought her a bowl of soup and more of the rolls.

'I fear so. It is wrong, of course, for the villagers to take and hide them, but they have suffered during the wars, as has most of Europe. Many of them lost sons and fathers, and the women find it difficult to manage.'

The money Fanny had given her had been in her small valise, carried inside the coach, in which she kept only the few things she would need on their overnight stops. It would have fallen out into the river, and probably floated, easy pickings for some lucky scavenger, and irretrievably lost to her. She was left with nothing apart from the clothes she wore, so how on earth was she to get herself and Maggie back to England?

She explained their dilemma to Sister Maria. 'And how can I repay you for all you have done for us?' she added.

'We do not ask for payment. It is our mission to care for the poor and sick and needy.'

'I could write to ask for more money to be

sent here,' Julia said slowly, 'but that would take a month or more. We cannot trespass on your hospitality for so long.'

'I wish we could give you the money for your journey, but we do not have so much to spare. Your friends will not be well enough to travel for some weeks. We can look after them meanwhile. You will have to apply to your friends for help.'

'There must be something more I can do!'

Sister Maria looked thoughtful. 'Are you willing to work, to earn money?'

'Here, in the convent? Of course! Anything.'

'Not here. But my brother runs an inn a few miles away. In the next town, along the same road you were travelling, a road much used by travellers from England. He would give you work, and you might find some compatriots who would either be of help to you, perhaps taking you with them back to England, so that you can then send money here for Maggie and Mr Williams, or taking a message to your sister, which would be more reliable than the posts.'

Julia jumped up from the bed and hugged Sister Maria. 'That's wonderful! I'll do anything. English people will be going home, for the Congress must be over soon.'

'I will ask for a message to be sent to my

brother this afternoon. Now you must rest, for you will not be well enough for even the lightest work if you do not.'

★ ★ ★

Three days later Julia was installed at the inn, working mainly in the bedrooms, and occasionally serving in the private parlours. She still felt weak, but forced herself to do the work without showing it. The innkeeper, Herr Ritter, insisted on paying her.

'I am glad of your help, for two of my maids are sick,' he told her.

Julia began to feel more cheerful. She had sent a letter to Fanny, asking her to send money to the convent for Maggie and Williams. If she could find some English people to help her, at least to take messages, she would. Letters could get lost in the post. In the few days she had been at the inn, no English travellers had passed through.

On the next evening Herr Ritter asked her to serve in the taproom, where he provided food as well as drink to the travellers who could not afford a private parlour. It was especially busy, she was told, and she had many trays to carry to the long table where the customers sat. By midnight she was exhausted, but a few men remained, drinking, and someone was still in one of the private parlours. Until they all left or went to bed she could not clear away their tankards and go to her own bed.

Then all but one of the men in the taproom left, and Julia went to collect the empty tankards. The man was slumped across the table, and she wrinkled her nose. She would never get used to the smell of beer in the taproom, but it was stronger here. She saw that one tankard had been knocked over, and the beer had run towards the edge of the table, where the man's sleeve was soaking it up.

'Have you finished, sir?' she asked. All the tankards were empty, and she hoped he would not want more.

She thought she heard the parlour door open and glanced across. Good, that guest was on his way to bed, and she would be able to clear away there as well.

The man on the bench glanced up at her, and a drunken smile spread over his face. 'Why, my dreams have come true,' he said, speaking in German and slurring the words so that she had difficulty in understanding him.

'Have you finished? May I clear away?'

'Here, pretty one. Come and get them. I've better things to do now.'

Like going home to your bed, Julia thought, and reached for the tankards nearest her. Then she jumped as he slapped her rump, and grabbing hold of her arm tried to drag her on to his lap.

'Let me go!' she demanded, trying to pull away from him, but he was strong and had a firm grip on her arm. She found herself falling forward, across his lap, and heard him chuckle as he put both arms round her.

'Give me a kiss, then,' he said, trying to twist her body so that her face was towards him.

Julia began to fight back in earnest, but the way he held her prevented her from kicking him, or scratching out his eyes, as she wanted to do. Then he released her so suddenly that she fell to the floor. By the time she struggled to sit up her tormentor and another man were fighting, staggering around and exchanging punches which rarely landed. They were equally drunk, Julia concluded, after watching them for a few moments.

She scrambled out of the way, for they were staggering wildly, knocking over stools. She eyed the pewter tankards, wondering whether she could use one as a weapon and hit the man who'd attacked her on the head, but before she could do so he received a blow on the chin which sent him crashing to the ground. Julia looked up to thank the other man, presumably her rescuer, but at that moment he slipped and fell himself, hitting his head on a corner of one of the benches.

By this time the commotion had brought others into the taproom. Herr Ritter took one look and ordered two of the pot boys to carry Julia's amorous swain outside, and put his head under the pump.

Another, plainly but well-dressed man had run to kneel by her rescuer.

'Oh, sir, pray wake up, do!' he said, in English, Julia noticed somewhere at the back of her mind.

Herr Ritter came across and helped the valet, for someone like that had to be a gentleman's gentleman, turn his master round.

'Fetch water and some cloths, girl,' Herr Ritter ordered, and Julia ran to the kitchen.

When she came back they had the man sitting up, resting against his valet's knee, groaning. His cravat had been loosened, and the valet was struggling to unwind it from his master's throat, saying distractedly that he must give him air.

'Better put a cold compress on that bruise,' Julia said, soaking one of the rags and holding it out. 'Move this cravat, I can't see where best to put it.'

Meekly the valet did as he was told, and Julia, leaning forward and about to apply the wet rag, almost dropped it in surprise. Her rescuer was Sir Carey Evelegh.

7

Julia found it impossible to sleep. She had been sent to bed by Herr Ritter, who said he and Tanner could carry the gentleman to his room. She supposed Sir Carey was on his way home, for this was a regular route many of the English visitors to Vienna had used. To meet him here should be no surprise, but to see him drunk was.

She had never seen him even mildly inebriated in Vienna, when they had been at balls where drink was freely available. Was he the sort of man who indulged when he was alone, but remained sober in company? Somehow that did not fit her image of him.

He had, however, saved her from the other man's unwelcome attentions. She could appeal to him for help in getting back to England. Then she paused. He might offer to escort her, but how could she possibly travel such a long distance alone with a man? She could not. It would ruin her reputation, and that was all she had. He might offer to lend her the money for the journey, and she could travel alone. Or he would take a message to Fanny, telling her the situation and asking for money to be sent here.

She was heavy-eyed by morning, and thankful she did not have to get up at dawn to wait on those guests who wanted to set off as soon as it was light enough to see their way. Herr Ritter, perhaps mindful of his sister's admonition to treat his temporary maidservant properly, had told her to sleep in when he sent her off to bed.

She was dozing when the thought that Sir Carey might be one of the travellers making an early departure caused her to sit up in alarm. Her tiny room overlooked the stable yard, and she had heard considerable activity there for some while, without thinking about it. The ostlers had been shouting, she had heard the stamping of horses' hoofs, and the sound of carriage wheels rolling over the cobbles. Was he the sort of man who could recover from drunkenness quickly? If so, he might have gone already, and she would have lost her best chance of help.

Hastily she dressed, dragged her hair back roughly with a ribbon, and covered it with the mob cap all the maids wore. Then she hurried downstairs.

As she entered the taproom Sir Carey's valet, who had been talking to Herr Ritter, turned and saw her.

'Oh, miss, my master wishes to speak to you.'

Julia gulped. 'Is he — better?' she asked, marvelling at a man's capacity to appear atrociously drunk, as well as suffer a blow on the head, and be up and apparently ready for conversation so early the following day.

The valet gave a discreet smile. 'My master does not indulge often,' he said, his voice prim. 'He has a severe headache this morning. From the blow to his head,' he added.

And she'd hazard a guess that wasn't the only cause, Julia thought, and then wished she had taken time to make her appearance tidier. She pulled the mob cap straight, and bit her lips, a trick she had seen Fanny use to redden them.

'The gentleman's in the parlour,' Herr Ritter intervened, and Julia nodded, and followed the valet towards the room indicated.

★   ★   ★

When Sir Carey awoke, his first thought was for his aching head, and his second a confused recollection that he had seen Julia Marsh bending over him the previous evening. Had it been a dream? Had she really been there, and if so, why? How had she come to be here? He'd seen no sign of anyone else from her party, no Lady Cunningham, no Mr or Mrs Pryce, no little girls. They had left Vienna several days before he had, and he would have expected them to be much further on the way home by now.

He gave up thinking about that. It was a puzzle he could not resolve by himself. His head ached abominably. He put his hand up to where the pain was most severe, and felt the bump on the side of his head. That was it. He remembered some fisticuffs. Why? Had he been attacked for some reason? That seemed unlikely within a respectable inn, and he had no recollection of going outside, where he might have been the object of robbery. His fighting was confined to Gentleman Jackson's rooms at number 13 New Bond Street, and he indulged more as a means of keeping in trim than because he was naturally bellicose.

There was a gentle tap on the door and Tanner put his head round it. 'Do you wish to get up yet, Sir Carey?' he asked. 'You did say you wanted to set off the moment it was light. That is, it was your intention last night, before you sustained your injury.'

Sir Carey groaned. 'Before I made a confounded fool of myself,' he said. 'Why was I fighting?'

Tanner came into the room. 'The man was molesting the young person,' he explained.

'She did not appear willing, so you knocked him down.'

'He must have knocked me down too, to cause this lump.'

'No, sir. There was beer on the floor, and you slipped, and hit your head on one of the stools.'

'I remember. And the girl? Was it she who was pressing cold cloths on my head?'

'Yes, sir, though the innkeeper soon sent her away so that he and I could put you to bed.'

Despite his headache, Sir Carey grinned. 'So you preserved my modesty?'

Tanner handed him a glass full of some white liquid. 'Drink this, sir. I found it very effective with my former master, who was one of the Prince Regent's intimates.'

'And went to bed roaring drunk every night?' Sir Carey commented, and after a disgusted look at the glass, took it and quickly drained the contents.

Half an hour later, feeling considerably better, he was downstairs in the parlour waiting for breakfast. He needed several cups of coffee to continue the good work Tanner's potion had started. Rolls and a few slices of beef and ham would be welcome, too, though he did not feel up to tackling eggs yet.

Then he recalled his dream of seeing Julia

Marsh. Had it been a dream? He could soon settle that, at least.

'Tanner, go and ask the girl who helped me last night to come here, please. I need to thank her.'

★ ★ ★

Fanny and the Pryces reached the coast more swiftly than they had expected, but had to wait two days for a passage. She had sunk into a dull lethargy, unable to think ahead or make plans.

'It is natural in your condition, my dear,' Elizabeth tried to reassure her. 'You are tired, you have been under considerable strain, and this journey has been long and tiresome. I am weary enough of it. But we will be in England soon, and then in London, where you will be able to rest.'

'You are very good to me. I wonder how far behind Julia is?'

'Not far, a few days only, I hope, and you may rely on Spicer and Williams to bring her and Maggie home as quickly as they can.'

'When they are with me again, I must make arrangements to go to Greystones. It's where Frederick will expect to find me if — when he comes home.'

'You need to rest, and you need cheerful

company, not moping alone in the country.'

Fanny shook her head. 'The Season will soon begin, and you will want to entertain, and go out to visit friends. I shall be in the way.'

'Nonsense. The house is big enough for you to have your own rooms, and you need never meet anyone if that is what you wish. We will send a message to Greystones so that Sir Frederick knows where you are.'

'You don't believe he will come back to me, do you?'

'Do you wish him to? After his behaviour?'

'I love him,' Fanny said, and began to cry. 'Besides, if this child should be a boy, I'll have given him his heir and he'll be delighted.'

'First you must look after yourself, so that you don't lose the baby. Moping in the country will do neither you nor him any good. If you are in London you can consult the best doctors, too.'

'You may have the right of it,' Fanny said. She was thoughtful. She desperately wanted this baby, not only for itself, but, if it should be a boy, as a means of bringing Frederick back to her.

'I do. The girls would not wish to be parted from my pair, either. They will miss their father less if they are with us. At Greystones they would notice his absence more.'

Fanny knew she was right. She would keep Julia with her, as governess, and soon Frederick would have realized his mistake, or his Russian mistress would tire of him, and he would come back to her.

★ ★ ★

Julia, thankful Sir Carey had not left, followed his valet into the parlour, and stood just inside the door, looking at him where he sat beside the fire, a table spread with several dishes drawn up before him. He looked pale, and his eyes were bloodshot. Were these signs of drunkenness, or something else?

'It was you! I thought I'd been dreaming. Julia, come and sit down. Tanner, send for more coffee. I want to know how the devil you come to be here, dressed like a servant.'

She couldn't suppress a smile. 'That's what I am, temporarily, Sir Carey,' she told him. 'A step lower than a governess.'

'Where is Lady Cunningham? And the Pryces? I was told you had all left Vienna together.'

'We did, but our coach was not so fast, and we lost touch,' Julia said, then paused as Herr Ritter himself came in with another pot of coffee and a cup and plate for Julia. He poured out some coffee and set the cup in front of her.

'Stay here with your friend,' the innkeeper said. 'Maybe he'll be able to help you.'

Sir Carey frowned. 'Of course, if I can. Thank you, Herr Ritter. Now,' he said, as the door closed behind the man and they were alone. 'You lost touch? Why did they not wait for you? This is most peculiar. Why should you need help? Why are you working here, at a wayside inn where, however respectable it seems, you are vulnerable to the sort of lascivious approaches I saw last night? And where are the others of your party?'

He carved her some ham, and Julia found she was hungry. She broke a roll and began to eat as she explained the arrangement of the two coaches.

'Then there was the accident, and Spicer, he was Mr Pryce's valet, was killed.'

'Killed? You poor girl! What accident?'

Julia, reluctant to recall those horrific moments, swiftly told him how the coach had foundered.

'We were taken to a convent and the nuns cared for us. Maggie is very ill with an ague. I was delirious with a fever for a day or so, but I soon recovered. Williams broke his leg and was taken to an abbey nearby. But we lost everything. I lost the money Fanny had given me for the journey. That's why I am here, hoping to find some English travellers who can at least take a message to Fanny and the Pryces.'

She did not add that she hoped to meet someone who might escort her back to England. If he offered, she could not accept.

There was a tap on the door, and Tanner appeared.

'I beg your pardon, miss, Sir Carey, but Frisby wants to know if he should put the horses to. Your baggage is all packed.'

'Then I'm afraid you'll have to unpack it. I'll need the carriage later, but not for an hour or so. Tell him we will not be leaving here today.'

Tanner bowed himself out, and Sir Carey turned back to Julia.

'Where is this convent? And the abbey? I will go and see how Maggie and the coachman are, and when they might be able to travel. Will you come with me, to vouch for me to the good nuns?'

★ ★ ★

They obtained directions to the abbey, and were carried there swiftly, despite the snow which was falling steadily.

Julia was shown to a small room where

125

there were just two chairs, being told courteously that women visitors were not permitted further. It was half an hour before Sir Carey came back and ushered her into his carriage.

'Williams is recovering, and very fretful. He blames himself very much for the accident to the coach, and Spicer's death, but I think I persuaded him these things happen, we cannot prevent all accidents. I have left sufficient money for him and Maggie to come home when they are well enough.'

Julia smiled at him. 'You are very kind, and Mr Pryce and Fanny will repay you when you get back to England.'

'There is no need.'

She was wondering whether he had left enough money for her as well, but finding it difficult to ask. 'I can go on working at the inn until they are better,' she said finally, and he turned to look at her.

'You can't stay there. It isn't fitting. We'll discuss what we are to do later, after I have seen Maggie.'

This time it was Sir Carey who was bidden wait, while Sister Maria led Julia to the small infirmary where Maggie was the only occupant.

To Julia's relief she was looking better, though she began to sob when she saw Julia.

'Oh Miss Julia, what's happening? No one

here can speak English and I can only understand a few words. I didn't know where you were, or Williams and Spicer, but whenever I try to ask, they shake their heads and pat my hands. I can't recall a thing, except I was so cold.'

Gently Julia told her about the accident to the coach, and how Williams had been injured but was recovering, and that Spicer had been killed.

Maggie closed her eyes briefly. 'I was getting fond of him,' she murmured. 'When can we go home? How shall we go?'

Not wanting to bother her with all the details, Julia merely said she had met Sir Carey, and he had made arrangements for them. 'Don't worry, as soon as Williams is fit to travel, we'll be going home. Meanwhile I have sent to let Lady Cunningham know the situation. And Sir Carey can tell her more when he arrives in London.'

⋆   ⋆   ⋆

By the time they were back at the inn the snow had stopped, and the sun was shining on the fresh snow. Julia thought how beautiful it was, the dark fir trees in the background, children playing and sliding on the frozen ponds, and the houses grouped round the main town square, where the gothic church stood opposite the inn.

Sir Carey ushered her in, and ordered food to be brought to the parlour. 'Now we must make arrangements for you,' he said. 'Will you stay with your sister when you get back to England?'

'I don't know,' Julia said with a sigh. 'We get on well enough, but if I teach the children she insists on paying me a wage, and I feel beholden. It would be bearable if Sir Frederick liked me, but I always feel he resents my presence, and I know he feels that I influence Fanny. She is older than I, but somehow she always asks my advice. Even if she doesn't always take it,' she added.

'Do you think he will give up this Russian Countess, and go back to her? Will she take him back?'

'Do wives have much option? She loves him, though. I'm certain she would welcome him back. Sometimes I could shake her for not being more assertive! She forgives him and he thinks he can do as he likes, so he never learns to treat her with proper respect. If I ever married, I would not endure such behaviour in a husband!'

He grinned. 'What would you do?'

Julia chuckled. 'Make his life so uncomfortable he'd soon regret his behaviour. However, that situation is unlikely to arise, so I must look for another position. As a governess this time, I think. I have enjoyed being with Alice and Paula.'

He said no more about how she was to get home, but chatted about the Congress, surmising that there would soon be a settlement.

'Lord Castlereagh will have reached England by now, I imagine,' Julia said wistfully. 'Is he really under pressure from Parliament? Don't they appreciate the difficulties of negotiating with men like the Tsar and the King of Prussia?'

'No, they don't. His lordship is not an eloquent speaker, not a man to sway the multitudes by his oratory. His public speeches are hesitant, uncomfortable, but I hope his sincerity will convince them.'

'You will be there for support.'

'I can do little but explain what the situation in Vienna has been. The problem is that most of our rulers care little for what happens in Europe, so long as England is secure from invasion, and Napoleon and his ambitions to conquer the world are confined in Elba.'

★   ★   ★

Julia was thankful to retire early. She had slept little the previous night, and it had been a stressful day. When she had sought out Herr Ritter and asked him what work he had for her, he had patted her hand and told her that now she had a protector she did not need to work for him.

'Besides, the two maids who have been sick are well enough to work again now.'

Julia chastised herself. She had been foolish to imagine the job here would be hers for as long as she wished. And she did not like the gleam in Herr Ritter's eye when he called Sir Carey her protector. Of course, the word in German might not carry the same implication as it did in English.

She was tired, but it was long before sleep claimed her. There were so many things she now had leisure to think about. She must brace herself to ask on the next day how he intended to help her get back to England. Much as she disliked the prospect, if he meant her to remain and come back with Maggie and Williams, she would need to ask for money to support herself while she waited. It was unlikely she would be able to obtain another job such as the one at the inn.

How was Fanny, she wondered? They must have reached England by now, and she hoped

Mrs Pryce had persuaded her to remain with them. If Fanny were left on her own for any length of time she was likely to fall into a lethargy.

Where was Frederick? Apart from having heard he was travelling towards Russia, she had not thought about him much. The Russian border was a long way from Vienna, almost as far as the Channel coast, and after that the country was endless. Where did Tania come from? Would she and Frederick go to her home? Or would they rather go to St Petersburg? For herself, she did not care in the least, but she cared for Fanny's sake. The further Frederick went, the more difficult he would find it to return to England, should he so wish. She giggled suddenly. What if Tania had grown tired of him, and he was deserted without funds? He probably hadn't thought of how he would support himself and Tania until he could make arrangements for money to be sent from his English bank. If he were stranded, not only would he have to provide for himself, but for his coachman and valet as well. She was grinning at the thought of Frederick working in an inn as a waiter when she finally fell asleep.

★　★　★

Sir Carey was wakeful too. He had put off the decision as to how Julia might be sent home. He was aware of what the gossips would say if he escorted her, with only the chaperonage of Tanner to protect her reputation. Maggie wasn't yet fit to travel, but he could not afford to linger much longer. He might hire a maid for her, but where would he find a suitable one? Would any suitable Bavarian girl want to travel to England? Or be sent back alone?

Then his thoughts returned, as they usually did when he had not drowned them with brandy, to Angelica's last letter. He had opened it with such pleasurable anticipation.

It was short and to the point, and he suspected it had been dictated by her mother, for the language was even more stiff and formal than he had become used to.

He had torn it up, but the words were imprinted on his mind, and every time he closed his eyes he could see them, in Angelica's round, childish handwriting.

My Lord, I write to Inform you that I wish to Terminate our Betrothal. I have met Another, who is more Likely to provide me with Enduring Happiness. We are to be wed Immediately. I remain, ever your Friend, Angelica.

Then at the bottom, in a hasty scrawl, she had written, *I trust you won't hate me.*

Had her formidable mother influenced her? He strongly suspected it. The woman had protested when he'd insisted his first duty was to support Lord Castlereagh in Vienna. Perhaps she had realized Angelica was fickle, susceptible to the admiration and flattery she had received during her début. Had she contrived to foster another betrothal, with an even richer suitor, or one with a more impressive title, during that house party Angelica had written she was so enjoying? Well, it seemed as though she had succeeded.

At first he had wanted to set off for England at once, but a few moments' reflection told him the letter had taken three weeks to reach him, and however hard he rode or drove it would take him two or more weeks to return to England. That was plenty of time for her mother to make sure Angelica was securely married, out of his reach. The deed was done.

He did his best to thrust thoughts of Angelica from his mind as he met with Lord Castlereagh and the Duke, but when his job of informally briefing the Duke was done, he set off for home. He had neglected his sisters for long enough, and they needed him even if Angelica did not. On the journey there was little to distract him, and he discovered the only way he could sleep was to drink brandy until Tanner was needed to put him to bed. Now he saw other possibilities and was more optimistic.

He was less heavy-eyed the following morning when he went down to breakfast. He had been thinking hard for much of the night, weighing the advantages of what he proposed against the inevitable problems, and finding the idea more attractive by the minute.

Julia, he discovered, had breakfasted in her room at Herr Ritter's command. 'For she is a guest now, is she not?' the innkeeper had told him, smiling widely.

'Please ask her to join me for some coffee,' he ordered briskly, and when Julia appeared a few minutes later, he rose to his feet and took her hand, leading her over to the table and pouring her some coffee. She'd removed her mob cap, and looked as ever neat and competent in her dark-blue gown, though he could see it had suffered, being limp and in places where the dye had run, discoloured.

He uttered polite, conventional remarks about hoping she had slept well, the weather seemed fair, some of the snow had gone during the night and the roads were said to be passable and free of ice.

She was sipping coffee when he looked at her and smiled.

'My dear, I have the solution to our problems. You need a job, I need a wife. Will you do me the honour of marrying me?'

8

'I'm being such a trouble to you,' Fanny sobbed. She was so worried she could not think straight. 'And where is Julia? And Maggie? They should be here by now. I can't abuse your hospitality any longer! I can't go on wearing your clothes!'

Fanny had just two dresses, which she had been carrying with her in the first coach, and she had been forced to borrow from Elizabeth. She refused to purchase more, saying her trunks would arrive when Julia did, and as she had so little money she did not wish to fritter it away until she knew how she stood.

'My dear Fanny, you know what Sir William Knighton said. He is the most respected doctor in London, the King's own physician, you must obey him. If you are to have any chance of carrying this child you must stay in bed. You can't go jaunting off to the country on your own. As to being a trouble, that's nonsense! We have a big house, and this suite of rooms used to be occupied by Edward's mother. It's almost a separate house, and it's been empty since she died.

And we have quite enough servants who, in general, don't have enough to do. It's the absence of Spicer that is causing most annoyance, and that only to my husband.'

'But the girls? I need to employ a governess for them, even when Julia returns. I cannot expect her to go on teaching them.'

'Miss Jenkins is quite happy to take on their education. She says it helps my pair to have others their age in the schoolroom. If it makes you feel better you could pay her something in addition to the salary we give her.' She paused, and coughed. 'My dear, this is rather delicate. Have you enough money? Did Sir Frederick make any provision for you?'

'He said he would arrange matters with his man of business. I have sufficient for now, as I have few expenses. Frederick arranged for the estate servants' wages to be paid, and the bills to be sent to Mr Podger while we were away. He will have dealt with them.'

'Then we will ask Mr Podger to call here and tell you what the position is, whether your husband has sent instructions. If he has not I'm sure Mr Pryce can convince him of the propriety of advancing what you need.'

Fanny gave her a watery smile. 'You are so good to me!'

Surely, she thought after Elizabeth had left

the room, they must hear soon from Julia. She was beginning to suspect there had been some accident. If it was some delay caused by, for instance, repairs being necessary to the coach, one of the party would have contrived to send a message. She needed her sister. Despite Elizabeth's kindness she felt so terribly alone.

★ ★ ★

Julia was busy mopping at the coffee she had spilt on her gown. Sir Carey must be inebriated again, though he showed no outward signs as he had on the evening he'd rescued her. Nothing else could explain his startling suggestion. For a brief moment her heart had leapt in astounded joy, then plummeted back to earth. It was not real. It must be a dream. She had misheard. Why on earth should he ask her to marry him?

He was already betrothed, she remembered, and had seemed very much in love with his Angelica. His eyes had lit up whenever he mentioned her.

Sir Carey had taken the coffee cup from her hand and set it down. He smiled ruefully at her.

'My fault, I fear. I rather startled you, I think. Miss Marsh, let me explain.'

He'd fallen into the habit of addressing her by her given name, so why this return to formality?

'You are already promised to Angelica,' she managed to say, her voice hoarse.

'Not any longer. She has married someone else. I don't even know who,' he added almost to himself, and Julia recognized the bleakness in his eyes.

'I'm sorry,' she said, and thought how inadequate these words were. 'But that does not mean you have to marry the first girl you see. Nor do you have to marry me to save my reputation. After Mrs Webber's tittle-tattling in Vienna it's a wonder I have any left.'

'No one believed her,' Sir Carey tried to reassure her.

'It's not just that. No one we know has any idea we are here in this inn. That we are both here is mere coincidence. A happy one for Maggie and Williams, I grant.'

She was babbling, and looked up at him in apology.

'I spent most of the night considering what best to do. Miss Marsh, Julia, I want to be frank with you, and I'll not pretend to any tender emotions. What I propose is more of a business arrangement than the sort of love match I thought Angelica and I enjoyed. I'll not deny that Angelica's defection has wounded me. I thought we were in love, but evidently her love was not as strong as mine.'

Julia shook her head, not in denial of his words, but at her own thoughts. If, incredible as it might seem, she did marry this man, she would have to conceal her own feelings. She could admit to herself now that she had from the start found him attractive. Her heart had always given a little jump when they met. But the sheer impossibility of anything other than mild friendship had made her clamp down on her emotions.

'That does not mean you have to marry,' she repeated.

'No, but I cannot imagine ever feeling for anyone else what I felt — still feel — for Angelica. There was another consideration. It did not sway my decision, but it would have been satisfying.'

He grinned, then rose and walked across to the fireplace, holding out his hands to warm them. 'My maternal grandfather was, to say the least, an eccentric. I was but three and twenty when my father died, and the old man, who maintained that all young men should be married to protect them from carnal temptation, left me his fortune on the condition that I must be married before I could enjoy it, and if I had not married by my thirtieth birthday, the money would go to my cousin, who had married when he was just twenty. The fact that my grandfather could not tolerate Daniel, and had not spoken to him for ten years, was irrelevant to him.'

'Is Daniel the man with the cats?' Julia asked.

'You recalled that?'

'I remembered the cats, after having avoided taking a position where I would have to groom them.' I can recall every word you ever said, Julia added to herself.

'Yes, he is,' Sir Carey went on. 'Of course, Grandfather was not to know that Daniel's wife left him a month of so after he died. I doubt he'd have approved. I did not care so much about the money, I am wealthy and have quite enough for my needs, and plenty to support my wife and provide for my sisters. But when I met Angelica and we fell in love I was amused that our marriage would deprive Daniel of Grandfather's legacy.'

'When are you thirty?' Julia asked.

'In the middle of July.'

'So you do not have a great deal of time to find a substitute wife,' Julia said.

'I was not looking for one. But I can see the advantages. Not just monetary, and the rather disreputable one of depriving Daniel of what he is expecting, but my sisters need someone older to guide them.'

'Why should you think I am qualified to do that?'

'You are of good birth, even if you have no money. I have watched and admired how you dealt with Lady Cunningham and her daughters. You will make an admirable wife. You have said you have little chance of marriage, apart from some impecunious curate. I can give you my name and my fortune, and in return you will act as my hostess and run my houses, and be an ideal companion to my sisters.'

'I — I need to think about it,' Julia said. 'Pray will you excuse me?'

'If it helps, I can promise you I will make no other demands on you,' he said quietly. 'I enjoy your company, but I will not insult you by pretending love for you. This would be a purely business arrangement.'

★   ★   ★

Julia wept unrestrainedly when she was safely in her tiny bedroom. This was a dream come true, and yet she could not accept. He did not love her, and never would. He would always be thinking of Angelica. And one day, whatever he thought now, his love for her might fade, and he might meet someone else he could love. She would be guilty of ruining his life if she agreed to his proposal and married him, so depriving him of possible future happiness.

Oh, but it hurt! To have glimpsed such bliss, even for just a few moments, and then know it would not be hers, was agony.

Gradually, as the storm of weeping lessened, she began to imagine what life could be like as his wife. There would be no more need to earn her living, no irritable old ladies to placate, or children to teach in houses where she would be neither family nor servant. Even if he did not love her, she would be with him, caring for his needs, making friends with his sisters and guiding them. It would not be enough.

Many marriages were purely business arrangements, she told herself. If the couples she had met in Vienna were all really in love with one another, why did so many of them enter into liaisons? Gossip was rife, not just in Vienna, but in England. Even some of the formidable patronesses of Almack's, those leaders of the *ton*, whose approval was so important in securing the success of any debutante, were rumoured to have been less than faithful to their husbands.

Her sleepless nights, together with the weeping, were too much. Julia fell asleep. It was dark when a knock on the door woke her.

'Yes? Come in,' she called out, looking in dismay at her crumpled and coffee-stained gown. It was Anna, another of the maids.

'Sir Evelegh, the gentleman you went out with yesterday, he asks you to join him for dinner in half an hour,' Anna said, and grinned conspiratorially. 'He is handsome, is he not?'

Julia nodded. She must be strong and give him his answer.

'Do you have a better gown?' Anna asked now. 'That one is too stained for dining with a gentleman.'

'It's the only one that was saved from the accident,' Julia said. 'What on earth can I do? There isn't time to wash it, even if the stain would come out. I'll have to press it and hope the stain doesn't show too much.'

'There isn't time. You could borrow my dress. It is the one we wear for festivals, but it is pretty. I think he will like you in it. I will fetch it.'

Before Julia could reply she had whisked away to her own room, across the narrow passage. Within a minute she was back, holding out one of the regional costumes like the ones Julia had admired in Vienna. The skirt was black, but brightly embroidered, and when Anne held it out Julia saw that there were several frilly petticoats which just showed beneath the hem. There was a blouse, white with more embroidery round the neck, and full sleeves, and a short cape, black again.

'Try it on. It should fit you, we are much of a size.'

Julia needed little urging. She had never worn clothes like this before, but anything was preferable to her stained and crumpled gown. The bodice had a low *décolletage*, but there were no strings for Julia to pull it up. When she tried to hitch it higher Anna playfully slapped her hand away.

'No, the gentlemen like to catch a glimpse of the attractions they hope to enjoy,' she said, giggling.

'It's not at all like that!' Julia protested. 'Sir Carey is merely an acquaintance who is helping me to get back to England. You know my situation, and the two people who are too ill to travel.'

'Of course,' Anna said, but could not suppress her amusement. 'I will take your old gown and clean it if I can. It will be ready for you in the morning.'

'You're very kind,' Julia said, and impulsively kissed the girl.

Anna giggled. 'Save your kisses for Sir Evelegh,' she advised. 'He will appreciate them!'

★ ★ ★

Sir Carey was dressing with more care than he had taken since he'd received Angelica's letter. He suspected he had made a mull of it. From Julia's reaction he judged she had not welcomed his proposal, and really, could he blame her? What girl would thank a man for telling her how much he had loved his former fiancée? Yet he had wanted to be truthful. He could not dissemble, and there had to be complete openness between them if they were to make a success of this odd marriage he was suggesting.

What further arguments could he employ? She was not mercenary. She would not accept him merely for the life he could provide, and to avoid the need to earn her own living. He respected her for that. He admitted he both respected and liked her. In other circumstances, if he had not met Angelica, and had been anxious to marry, he could easily have settled for her. Julia would not treat him to tantrums and the vapours whenever they had some disagreement.

He recalled her remark that she would find ways to punish a wayward husband, and smiled in amusement. He had no doubt she would have some ingenious notions. But even though their marriage would be a business affair, he would never subject her to the sort of gossip her sister had to endure.

Where was Sir Frederick? Was he still with his new mistress? Had they reached Russia, and what did he make of that country? It was not an easy country to understand, and he doubted Sir Frederick had the mental capacity to see beneath the surface of the Russian people, with their almost childlike ability to express their emotions without any reserve.

He supposed, if he married Julia, he would be expected to take an interest in her sister. That would not be impossible. He thought Fanny a pleasant, if weak woman, but the little girls were well mannered, easy to be with.

He cast aside yet another cravat. Why could he not tie one properly? Surely he was not nervous! He had not been nervous when he proposed to Angelica. But he'd known she would accept him, she'd shown her liking for him from the moment they'd met. Her father had welcomed the match, saying bluntly she was a giddy chit and needed a sensible older man to control her starts. It was her mother who, Sir Carey suspected, wanted a higher title for her daughter.

Julia's acceptance could not be taken for granted. She had not appeared in any way pleased at his proposal, and perhaps it served him right for introducing the matter so abruptly. But he was anxious to get home, and surely she was too. They could be married here, and set off within a few days. He must, somehow, persuade her of the sense of his proposal.

★　★　★

Mr Podger was tall and thin, not at all as his name had suggested to Fanny. Mr Pryce had asked him to call at the house to advise Fanny. She had not met him before, and although he was never less than professional, she had the impression he was sympathetic to her and condemnatory towards Frederick.

She had refused to see him while she was in bed, and despite Elizabeth's reassurances that it would not be thought at all improper, she insisted on donning a loose robe and meeting him in the small but well appointed boudoir attached to her bedroom. Elizabeth, at Fanny's pleading, sat with her and held her hand encouragingly.

'Lady Cunningham,' he intoned. There was no other word for it, she thought, striving not to giggle. Somehow her spirits lifted, and she smiled without any effort as she bade him take a seat.

After carefully inspecting the comfortable chairs scattered about the room he chose the hardest, which had been set before a small writing table. He turned it round and placed it six feet away from Fanny, then sat down.

'I have to inform you I have not heard anything from your husband,' he said. 'However, in the circumstances I feel it my duty to ensure you and the children are not placed in a difficult situation. I am sure that is what Sir Frederick would wish, if his wishes could be known.'

'Thank you,' Fanny said. She was not at all sure what Frederick's wishes would be, in his present state of infatuation with his Russian lover.

'I intend to make you a quarterly allowance, to cover all your expenses, and those of the children. The bills for your household and Greystones will, of course, continue to be sent to me, and I will deal with them. The allowance is comparable to what you were accustomed to receive as pin money, enlarged in order to allow for any unforeseen charges you might face.'

He named a sum which left Fanny gasping. It was twice the pin money and dress allowance she had received from Frederick. She gave him a puzzled look, and he smiled briefly.

'You will have unexpected expenses which, in normal circumstances, if Sir Frederick were here, he would pay. Such as hiring a carriage, when you can drive out, or to go to Greystones. However, if it is insufficient, you need only ask and I will arrange for the allowance to be increased.'

'It's too much,' Fanny began, but Elizabeth interrupted.

'Much too good of you, Mr Podger, and Lady Cunningham is most grateful. If there are any problems you do not care to bother Lady Cunningham with, my husband will be only too pleased to do whatever is needful.'

Fanny saw them look each other in the eye for a silent few seconds, and then Mr Podger smiled.

'I think that is all, ladies, so I will take my leave.'

★ ★ ★

Julia, feeling horribly conspicuous in Anna's brightly coloured clothes, went swiftly downstairs and into the parlour. When Sir Carey looked up and smiled, she detected amusement in his face.

'I can't help it!' she exclaimed. 'My gown had coffee stains on it, and isn't fit for polite company. Anna, one of the other maids, lent me this.'

'So at least you admit I am polite

company,' he said, and laughed aloud. 'You look charming, my dear. Come and sit here beside the fire. It grows chilly tonight. I think we can expect a frost.'

Julia went where he indicated, and he sat on the chair opposite, the table between them.

'Do you have just the one gown?' he asked.

'All my luggage was lost in the river,' she reminded him. 'Fortunately I was wearing my cloak, which the nuns cleaned and dried for me.'

'Of course, I hadn't remembered. That must be making life very difficult for you.'

She shrugged. 'Yes, but many peasants have only one gown. I have grown accustomed to it.'

He looked at her steadily for a few moments, then walked towards the door.

'Excuse me one moment. I need to speak to Herr Ritter.'

It was several minutes before he returned, followed by two maids bearing several platters and dishes. They set the table briskly, and then, bobbing a curtsy to Julia, retreated.

She felt embarrassed. Until two days ago she had worked alongside these girls. They had been wary of her at first, until they realized she worked as hard as any of them.

'This looks like an excellent chicken. Will

you have some?' Sir Carey asked. 'Or do you prefer some of the pie? It's rabbit, I think. Have you developed a taste for the German sausages? I cannot say I appreciate them.'

'A little chicken, please,' Julia managed. They would eat first, apparently, and not introduce the matter between them. Later, she would tell him all her reasons. He had been honest with her, and deserved her own honesty. Apart from one thing, she hastily amended. She could never admit to him that she had any softer feelings for him.

Somehow she managed to eat what he gave her, and drink a glass or two of wine, though she refused most of the dishes. He ate heartily, and all signs of his recent indulgence in brandy had vanished. Herr Ritter himself came in to clear the table when they were finished, and bring a pot of coffee. Sir Carey waved away the decanter.

'I don't want that,' he said. 'Can you see we are not disturbed again?'

'Of course. Ring the bell if you require anything else.'

Julia clasped her hands together in her lap. She had to make him understand.

'Well?' he asked softly. 'Have you considered my suggestion?'

'I cannot accept,' Julia burst out. 'It would not be fair to you. One day you might meet someone else you might love, and then I would stand in your way.'

'I did not think there was anyone else you had a *tendre* for,' he said. 'You need not be concerned that I will ever fall prey to the softer emotions again. And I promise you I will never mention Angelica again. It would be churlish to keep reminding you, but I had to explain. It isn't as though reminders would distress you, since we are not young lovers, but it would not be fitting. That part of my life is over, and I want us to make a fresh start. We seemed to have interests in common while we were in Vienna, did we not?'

Julia nodded, unable to speak.

'I admire and respect you, and I do not think you have some antipathy to me?'

He looked a question, and she shook her head.

'Then could we not make a success of a business arrangement?'

Julia could remain seated no longer. Impetuously she rose to her feet and began pacing the room. 'Don't you understand?' she cried. 'I would be ruining you! What would people say, when you marry a penniless girl so soon after being jilted? You must take time to consider, you must!'

He stepped in front of her and grasped her arms. 'Quietly, Julia! Do you care what people say? It's no one's business but ours. We met in Vienna, and got to know one another there. That is the truth, and all people need to know.'

The door opened and he turned round, about to tell whoever it was to leave. The words died on his lips as a couple he had met in Vienna, Mr and Mrs Webber, entered the room. Herr Ritter hovered anxiously behind, muttering that the gentleman did not wish to be disturbed.

'La, no wonder! What have we disturbed? Is this a rural idyll?' Mrs Webber asked and tittered. 'Gregory's valet met yours upstairs, and we were told you were here. There isn't another private parlour to be had, so I told Gregory you would surely not object to sharing yours with benighted travellers.'

Sir Carey's hands had tightened on Julia's arms as she tried to pull away. She belatedly recognized the woman as the one who had been at Fanny's party when Paula had been unable to sing, and she was almost certain she had been one of the women who had not bothered to conceal their laughter.

Mrs Webber came into the room, and peered curiously at Julia. 'What a pretty costume, dear. Is it fancy dress? But don't I know you? Aren't you — let me see, don't you teach Lady Cunningham's children? Of course, you're the girl they were all talking about in Vienna. I suppose they'll all have forgotten whatever you did in England to cause such a stir, and it's possible for you to return there. Is Lady Cunningham here too?'

'I have nothing to fear, and never did, in England, Mrs Webber. The gossip in Vienna was all malicious lies, and I think I know who started it. As for my sister, she is, I hope, in London by now,' Julia said through gritted teeth.

Mrs Webber smiled, and it reminded Julia of a cat's sly glance. 'And she has left you alone with Sir Carey? Doesn't she care about your reputation, child?'

'Julia's reputation is perfectly safe with me,' Sir Carey said, putting one arm round Julia's shoulders and pulling her towards him. 'We are betrothed, and are to be wed in the morning.'

9

Julia opened her mouth to deny it, but Sir Carey's hand on her shoulder gripped her in warning.

Mrs Webber looked startled, then smiled in comprehension.

'I see,' she said, her voice full of insinuation. 'The gentleman has noble instincts. I don't know how you came to be here alone with him, but he is doing the right thing to protect your name. Or is he? Is this just a pretence to put me off? We'll soon see when we all get back to London.'

'Allow me to tell you that you are being offensive, ma'am,' Sir Carey said. 'And now, perhaps, Herr Ritter will make sure you are served dinner in your bedroom, as this parlour is reserved for me and my guests.'

'Well, really! Allow me to tell you, sir, that I shall make it my business to let everyone know how this penniless trollop managed to snare a wealthy husband!'

With that she swept out of the room, her husband following meekly. Herr Ritter gave them an apologetic shrug and closed the door.

Julia moved away from Sir Carey and sank on to a chair. 'She will, you know, she's an odious gossip. What are we to do?'

'Get married, as I said. I've made enquiries and there is a pastor willing to perform the ceremony tomorrow.'

'But I don't want to!'

'If your reasons are the ones you stated before that wretched woman interrupted us, then they don't hold water, my dear. I shall never again allow myself to fall in love. It was a mistake, and I have come to accept that a business arrangement with someone who is pleasant, capable, and calm, is preferable to one where the initial violent attraction is likely to fade, leaving nothing in its place.'

Julia sighed. 'You think that now, but you would regret it in a few years.'

'I promised not to mention Angelica again, but I must, in order to convince you. She is pretty, and lively, and could have married anyone. She had plenty of offers. For me it was an instant attraction, and I was like a green boy again, in thrall to her, overwhelmed when she showed a preference for me. However, since I have been away from her I have gradually, without really understanding it, begun to think she is rather shallow, and does not care for any of the more serious concerns.'

'She's very young,' Julia interrupted. 'She will come to care for them, if she wants to please you. You cannot judge her solely by her letters. Many girls find it difficult to express themselves adequately.'

'You forget, she will be out of my reach by now, so this is not a possibility. I think she has saved me from making a big mistake. I've no doubt she has been trained to run a house efficiently, or at least to order the servants to do so, but I am becoming more and more convinced that we would never have been companions, in the way I would wish to have companionship with my wife. It is not just the letters, I have been thinking back to when we were together, remembering, and trying to ignore the unease I felt, telling myself it would be all right once we were married or when she was older. If I face the truth, I know it would not have been.'

'But you can't know that you and I would deal well together!'

'I'm now convinced we would have a more successful marriage than I and Angelica ever could have done. My dear Julia, you will not change my mind.'

'You're not taking heed of my wishes!'

'You have no prior attachment. Your life, without a dowry, would be a succession of unsatisfactory positions living as a dependant in other people's houses. Unless you found an indigent curate,' he added, and Julia felt her heart beating rapidly at that devastating smile. 'I can give you a position in society, a country house, a hunting box, a house in London, and ample pin money. All I want in return is your companionship, your help in managing my houses, and your guidance for my sisters, who will be married and away from Courtlands within a few years. Is that not a better prospect than being a companion to elderly, probably crotchety old ladies, or a governess to spoilt children?'

It was so tempting. Julia knew it would not be a complete marriage, but just to have his company would be enough.

She sighed. 'I trust I will not prove you wrong. Very well, Sir Carey, I will accept your proposal.'

★ ★ ★

Sir Carey breathed a sigh of relief. He was sincere in his arguments, but he also knew that if they did not wed her reputation would be in tatters. Julia would probably insist she took no heed of what the world said about her, but he found he cared enough for her to protect her from society's condemnation.

He walked across to the table and poured

out two more glasses of wine. Handing one to her he lifted his own high. 'To us, Julia.'

They drank, and found there was little to say. They were both, he decided, somewhat astonished at the speed of events. Then Julia, rather hesitantly, took a deep breath and spoke.

'Tell me about your home, please. It is named Courtlands, I believe?'

'Yes, it is in Oxfordshire. It started as a small Norman castle, then another wing was built on in the 1670s after the Restoration. They knocked down most of the medieval buildings. My grandfather put on a new frontage and two wings, in the classical style. It's an architectural disaster, but we all love it.'

Julia laughed. 'It sounds fascinating.'

'You'll love it too,' he said, and watched her eyes cloud over.

Was he doing the right thing, forcing her in this way? If she had any realistic opportunity of a suitable marriage he'd have hesitated. He thought they would deal together admirably, but had he taken her feelings sufficiently into account? He'd used the opportunity presented when Mrs Webber came into the room and found him holding Julia's arms. She had misinterpreted the situation, probably imagining they had been embracing. Chivalry would have demanded he offer Julia his hand, but he'd already done that.

They had to go through with it now, ready to face the gossips when they returned to London. He'd drive through the night, and make sure he reached England and made his marriage known by sending a notice to *The Times* before the malicious Webbers reported the facts with all the inaccurate embellishments they were capable of.

'We'll be up early tomorrow,' he said. 'Can you pack tonight? I'd like to set off as soon as the ceremony is over. We should try to reach London before the Webbers.'

Julia smiled rather grimly, and nodded. Yes, he'd not underestimated her intelligence. She had clearly seen the wisdom of this at once, and having accepted the situation, seemed determined to make the best of it.

'I'll say goodnight, then, sir. As to packing, all I have is my coffee-stained gown. I'm afraid I shall not do you justice in my wedding dress!'

★　★　★

Anna was in Julia's room, and turned to her in excitement when Julia went in.

'This is only a small town, but I managed to find a few gowns and nightclothes, and a fur-lined pelisse and hat. I even found some oil of jasmine Sir Evelegh said he particularly

161

wanted you to have, as you lost yours in the accident,' she said proudly, holding out a small glass phial.

Julia blinked back tears. How thoughtful of him, and how clever of him to have known the perfume she preferred.

'I bought a trunk to pack them in,' Anna said, 'and I threw your old gown away, it was impossible to get the stain out. Look, this one will do for your wedding dress, and it is warm enough for you to travel in tomorrow. Sir Evelegh said you were leaving at once after the ceremony. A pity, we'd all have liked to wish you well. But Herr Ritter says that anyone not working can attend the wedding, if you don't object.'

Julia could not speak. The bed was covered in clothes. The gown Anna was holding up was a warm woollen one in a delicate shade of rose. The pelisse was a darker shade, trimmed with sable, and the hat, close-fitting and also trimmed with fur, was of an identical shade. There were gloves, a sable muff, some half boots of black kid, plus a small black leather reticule. A fur-lined cloak in service-able black was draped over the only chair.

'Don't you like them?' Anna asked anxiously. 'Sir Evelegh gave me so much money, and told me to buy the best the town could provide.'

'I'm overwhelmed,' Julia said, blinking back tears. How incredibly thoughtful of Sir Carey. 'I was not looking forward to getting married in my old gown!'

'It's all so romantic,' Anna babbled on, as she folded the clothes and packed them into the trunk. 'Fancy you knowing him in Vienna, and him turning up here without knowing you were also here.'

Julia was stroking the fur of the muff, then she held it to her cheek. It was not romantic in the way Anna meant, but it was dreamlike. She had been attracted to Sir Carey from the start, but had never thought he might make her an offer, even before she heard about his betrothal to Angelica. If only he felt more than mild liking for her! He'd overborne her objections, and she had no option but to marry him. She could only hope they would neither of them regret it in the future.

* * *

The actual wedding ceremony passed in a blur. Julia, wearing the pretty rose-coloured dress, made her responses in German when prompted, but afterwards could remember nothing until the pastor, a jolly, round-faced little man, nodded and beamed at them.

'You may kiss the bride,' he said in heavily

accented English, and chortled.

The sound of quiet laughter made Julia glance over her shoulder. Several of the servants from the inn were present, and when Sir Carey turned her towards him and took her in his arms, they broke into applause.

He pulled her to him and bent towards her. Mutely she stared as his face came closer, and gasped in surprise as his lips, warm and soft, descended on her own.

It seemed an eternity before he drew back, smiling. 'Thank you, Lady Evelegh,' he said, almost in a whisper.

Julia wanted to touch her lips. Not to wipe away the unexpected kiss, but with the foolish idea that if she covered them up she would continue to feel the frisson of excitement which had overwhelmed her.

'The carriage is ready, Sir Carey, and fully provisioned as you ordered,' Herr Ritter said, breaking the tension.

Sir Carey took Julia's arm and led her to where the carriage was waiting, with Frisby and another man, a stranger, sitting on the box. Tanner stood holding the open door, and Sir Carey, pausing to say a few words of thanks, ushered Julia inside. Tanner climbed in after them and sat on the forward seat, as far as he could away from them, trying to look inconspicuous.

There were hot bricks wrapped in cloths to warm their feet, and several thick rugs to tuck round them. Sir Carey clearly travelled in as much comfort as could be managed.

Julia waved to the people who had come to see her off, and saw several more of the inn servants standing on the steps. Behind them, glowering, were Mr and Mrs Webber.

'Good, we've a start on them,' Sir Carey said, sounding satisfied. 'Julia, I've hired a second coachman as far as the coast. I plan to drive through the night most of the time, so that we may reach London first. Don't worry, the carriage is well-equipped, I had it specially built for travelling when I went to Russia, where one cannot always find inns. You will be able to sleep in comfort.'

Julia glanced quickly at Tanner, who was sitting with downcast eyes. Was he thinking this was an odd way of spending a wedding night? But she was relieved. Sir Carey had promised he would make no demands on her, and from that she had assumed they would occupy separate bedrooms. This might be impossible if the inns they stayed at were crowded.

She took a deep breath and turned to smile at him.

'I'm sure I will, Sir Carey.'

★ ★ ★

It took them eight days to reach the coast. Sir Carey told Julia that the couriers between London and Vienna, riding hard, could sometimes make the journey in two weeks. They spent two nights at inns, and to Julia's relief they had been able to hire suites with a parlour and separate bedrooms. As Sir Carey had said, his carriage was well equipped to provide them with comfortable beds. Their seats could be pulled forwards so that they could lie flat, and Tanner, with whichever coachman was not driving, curled up on the forward seat. Once Julia became accustomed to sleeping in the same small space as three men, she found the rocking of the carriage lulled her to sleep.

Sir Carey was always concerned with her comfort. At each halt for food or to change the horses he insisted on more warm bricks being brought to place under Julia's feet, so that she was protected from the bitter cold. Sometimes, at the start, they ate as they drove along. Herr Ritter had packed a lavish hamper, with pies and cold fowl, hard boiled eggs, even some smoked trout, as well as loaves and cakes and some small, wrinkled apples. There were bottles of wine and brandy, and one of champagne. There seemed enough for the whole journey, Julia thought, but Sir Carey decreed they needed to eat a proper meal occasionally, sitting beside warm fires and at tables like civilized people. These breaks allowed Julia to stretch cramped limbs, take brief walks to see the sights in the towns where they stopped, and be ready for several more hours of travel.

Tanner's presence inhibited private conversation, and Sir Carey confined himself to describing Courtlands and the surrounding countryside in more detail. Julia once said she felt she could find her way about it without a guide, and Sir Carey laughed.

'I challenge you!' he said. 'When we arrive I will send you in alone, with a list of the rooms to visit.'

He seemed more light-hearted than when Julia had known him in Vienna. Perhaps it was because he was not involved in the political negotiations, worrying about the outcome. Perhaps it was the thought of soon coming home. She dared not attempt to hope it was her own presence.

That changed when they were fifty miles from the coast. They stopped at an inn for dinner, to find a flag showing the Imperial Eagle flying from one of the windows.

'That's deuced odd,' Sir Carey commented. 'Have we found some of Napoleon's supporters? It's not everyone who relishes the return of the Bourbons, but I wasn't aware the Emperor's supporters were so open about it.'

They soon discovered the reason when they entered the inn.

'Napoleon is back!' an elderly man sitting in the taproom told them, waving a tankard at them. 'He's escaped from Elba, and he's marching on Paris. We'll soon send Louis packing!'

★ ★ ★

'It's bad,' Sir Carey told Julia half an hour later. He had installed her in a private parlour and gone out to glean what reliable news he could.

'Is it true?'

'He landed in the south a week ago, and is marching towards Paris. It appears no one is able, or willing, to stop him.'

'So the fighting will start all over again?' she asked. 'We have been at war almost all my life.'

'He can't possibly gather yet another army. He's taken all the young men, and the losses have been terrible in Spain and Russia, as well as many other campaigns.'

'Will the Congress end now? Is there any

use in continuing to negotiate while no one knows what the situation will be like in a few months?'

'We'll have to see. But it must have been rank incompetence that let him get away from Elba. Metternich warned at the time he was sent there it was too near France, and there would be another war within two years. He's been proved right. It's taken less than a year.'

★   ★   ★

They reached London three days later, and drove straight to Sir Carey's house in Upper Brook Street.

'Will the servants be expecting you?' Julia asked, afraid they would find the shutters up and no preparations made.

'They'll be expecting me,' he said, chuckling. 'I sent a message as soon as the Duke arrived in Vienna, for I knew I'd be coming home soon.'

His face grew sombre for a moment, and Julia recalled he would have been coming home for his wedding to Angelica.

'You'll be a surprise to them, though,' he added, and smiled at her.

'I ought to let Fanny know I am safe,' Julia said. 'Even if my letters did reach her, she'll be so worried about me. And I have to explain how all the baggage was lost, and — and about Maggie and the Pryces's servants.'

'You can write her a note, someone will take it to the Pryces' house. I expect she'll still be with them, but if not I'll send one of the grooms down to Greystones with it.'

'May I go and see her tomorrow?' she asked.

'Of course, my dear Julia. You are to do exactly as you wish.'

'But if you need me, as hostess,' Julia added quickly, 'or to meet your friends, you must tell me and I will not arrange anything else.'

'I will tell you,' he promised, 'but you are not my servant. You will soon have your own friends and your own life to lead, here and at Courtlands.'

So he expected her to lead an independent life, did he? Well, she had no right to expect anything else.

'We have an agreement,' she told him. 'I am to be your hostess and run your houses.'

'I'm sure you will do it admirably. Here we are.'

It was a tall, narrow house, and as the carriage drew up at the door it opened to reveal a stout, elderly butler who beamed at Sir Carey.

'Welcome home, sir,' he said. 'We've been expecting you for some days now.'

Sir Carey leapt down and turned to hand Julia from the carriage. 'I delayed in order to get married, Foster,' he said. 'Meet Lady Evelegh. Julia, Foster has been with the family since before I was born. If you need to know anything, just ask him.'

Julia had to admire Foster's imperturbability. There was not even a flicker of surprise crossing his face. She wondered if they all knew about Angelica. No doubt there had been gossip and speculation when Angelica's marriage to someone else had been announced.

Sir Carey led her into the hallway, the floor chequered in black and white marble, and an elegant staircase curving away at the far end. He opened a door on the right and ushered her into a small parlour which overlooked the garden at the rear of the house.

'Lady Evelegh has no maid, Foster. Can you suggest one who could help her until we have time to hire one?'

'I think Molly will suit, sir. Where shall I have the baggage taken?'

'Have Lady Evelegh's put in my mother's old room. Tanner knows which is hers. It's in order?'

'Always, sir.' Foster seemed offended at the question, and Julia tried not to smile.

From what she could see the house looked clean, the rugs swept, and the furniture polished. There were, though, no ornaments, no flowers such as Fanny always had, and the curtains were faded. The paintings in this room were of poor quality and undistinguished. The couple she'd glimpsed in the hall, of gentlemen in Elizabethan costume, were presumably ancestors, but there was so much varnish which had darkened with age it was difficult to see any features. The house had lacked a woman's touch for too long.

'I shouldn't have asked! You are always efficient. We'll have a light supper in the morning-room, while our baggage is unpacked. Have someone ready in a few minutes to deliver a note.'

★ ★ ★

Fanny was asleep when Julia's note was delivered, so did not read it until her breakfast tray was brought to her. Recognizing Julia's handwriting she tore open the note, and scanned it swiftly, then burst into tears of relief.

'Thank goodness! She's alive and well! Please ask Mrs Pryce to come here as soon as she is dressed,' she told the maid.

When Elizabeth, in a dressing-gown,

entered the room a few minutes later, looking anxious, Fanny thrust the letter into her hands.

'Fanny, what is it? You have a high colour. You mustn't excite yourself. Is something wrong?'

'No, but this is from Julia. She's in London, and she's well. But she says she had to leave Maggie and Williams behind, there was an accident. Oh, why does she give no more details, and where on earth is she staying? She can't have had the audacity to go to a hotel by herself, surely? Even Ibbetson's is not suitable for a single young lady. And did she travel by herself? Why did she not come here? She could have guessed I'd still be with you.'

'Fanny, don't fret, you'll make yourself ill. We will soon know.'

Elizabeth straightened out the sheet of paper and read it slowly. 'How very odd,' she commented. 'She's written it on headed notepaper, and I know that address. It's where Sir Carey Evelegh lives.'

Fanny sat up abruptly. 'Sir Carey? How does she come to be with him? What has she done now? She'll be ruined if anyone else hears about this. Oh, Elizabeth, will you send someone round at once and ask her to visit me immediately? I shall die of frustration if I don't discover what this is all about soon!'

It was an hour later when Julia entered Fanny's bedroom. She went across to her sister and they hugged convulsively, and Fanny burst into tears.

'I have been so worried!' she sobbed. 'Where have you been all this time? What's all this about an accident?'

'I wrote. Did you not get any of the letters?'

'No. Julia, what happened?'

Julia explained. 'So Maggie won't be here for a while. And she may find it difficult to travel now Napoleon is gathering another army. I'm thankful Williams will be with her. He's sensible and will look after her.'

'He doesn't appear to have looked after you when he let a wheel fall off the coach! Poor Maggie.'

Fanny was genuinely sorry for her maid, she was fond of the girl, who was cheerful and efficient, but she was more concerned with what sort of coil her sister was in.

'Now, Julia, what in the world are you doing at Sir Carey's house? Is he there with you? You mustn't let people know. You must come here at once. Elizabeth is preparing a room for you. Why didn't you come here?'

Julia sat down on a chair beside the bed, and was straightening the fingers of her gloves. Very good quality gloves, Fanny thought, and now she had time to notice, so were Julia's pelisse and dress, as well as being new, better quality than she was accustomed to wearing.

'Elizabeth tells me you are breeding, and the doctor insists you stay in bed,' she said. 'How are you feeling?'

'Better than I did at first. The jolting and swaying of the coach was dreadful, of course.'

'Have you heard from Frederick?'

Fanny shook her head. She both longed for her husband to come back to her, and was furious with him for the way he had deserted her.

'Not a word. Julia, tell me at once why you are staying at Sir Carey's house! You haven't done anything foolish, I hope? But I didn't think he was that sort of man.'

'I'm not sure if it's foolish of me or not,' Julia said slowly. 'Fanny, he asked me to marry him, and I said yes, and we were married in Bavaria.'

10

Julia was exhausted by the time she left Fanny. Her sister had demanded every detail of the journey, pressed repeatedly for assurances that there had been nothing improper between her and Sir Carey which had forced his hand, and exclaimed about Angelica's defection in words which Julia, amused, thought rather disparaging to herself, even if she privately agreed with them.

She had thought it expedient not to reveal the real nature of the marriage, for that would have set Fanny off again in further speculations.

On the way back to Upper Brook Street she bought some flowers. From what she had glimpsed of the garden there, it would provide nothing but dark green ivy, and some cheerful spring blossoms would do much to brighten the house.

Foster greeted her politely, and informed her that Sir Carey had gone into the City to see his man of business.

'Shall I send Molly to you, my lady?'

'Please. And is there anywhere I can arrange these? Do we have some vases?' she

176

asked as he took the flowers from her.

'There is a cupboard near the kitchen where they are stored,' he said. 'I suggest I prepare the morning-room and have some water sent there for you. We do not have a flower room here as we do at Courtlands. My lady, Sir Carey's mother, used to be fond of arranging flowers, and it will be good to see some in the house,' he added.

'Thank you. I will be down as soon as I have changed.'

Molly appeared within a minute of Julia reaching her bedroom. She was a rosy-cheeked country girl, with slow drawling speech but a ready laugh, and Julia had taken to her immediately. The previous evening she had unpacked and stowed Julia's new clothes swiftly and efficiently.

'Molly, what is your position here?'

'Head housemaid, my lady.'

'Would you like to be my personal maid?'

Molly's eyes widened, and she nodded eagerly. 'I would that, but I'm not sure Mrs Carter would let me.'

'Mrs Carter?'

'The housekeeper, here and at Courtlands, my lady. Real strict, she be, with us maids. When she put me up to head housemaid, when Janie left, she warned me I had to prove myself or I'd be back where I started.'

Julia raised her eyebrows. Mrs Carter sounded like a strict disciplinarian. 'How long have you held the position?'

Molly counted on her fingers. 'Let me see, it were October Janie left to be wed, so it's five months.'

'Then you must have given satisfaction.'

'Well, mebbe so, but as she said this morning, with Sir Carey back, and with a wife, there'll be more to do, and she'll be watching me. She said you'd most like be entertaining. Sir Carey didn't do much.'

'Does Mrs Carter hire all the servants?'

'The maids, yes. Mr Foster hires the men.'

'I see. Well, I've a mind to choose my own personal maid, and if you want to, you can have the position.'

'Ooh, my lady! Thank you! I didn't expect to have such a job for years,' she confided.

Julia smiled. 'I'm sure we'll get on. I'd prefer to have someone used to the household than a newcomer.'

★   ★   ★

The cupboard where the vases were stored was also crammed with ornaments, vases and figurines, some of which, to Julia's inexpert eye, looked valuable.

'Why are they here?' she asked Foster.

'When his lordship's father died, he ordered everything to be put away. As he was not expecting to be here a great deal, and the house would be shut up for many months, I think he wanted to give the caretaker and his wife less work. I also suspect he doubted the woman's ability to dust them without breakage.'

'It's a pity to shut them away. When I've done the flowers I'll come back and find a few to brighten up the rooms.'

She was humming softly to herself an hour later as she positioned two Meissen figures on the drawing-room mantel-piece. When she turned to leave the room she saw Sir Carey in the doorway, smiling.

'I hope you don't mind?'

'The house somehow looks more cheerful already, my dear. Of course I don't mind. This is part of our bargain.'

She explained about Molly. 'I hope I did right. Mrs Carter seems to think I should have consulted her before interfering with her arrangements. I will do so in future.'

He frowned. 'Was she impertinent? I won't tolerate that.'

'No, just aggrieved.'

'You have every right to hire whomever you wish as your maid, and to dismiss anyone if you feel it necessary.'

Julia smiled in relief. 'Thank you. I do not wish to be at odds with your housekeeper, but I wasn't sure of my authority.'

'Absolute, as far as the house is concerned. If you feel it needs refurbishing, you have only to say so.'

'I'd like to banish those gentlemen in the hall to some dark corner,' she confessed. 'They look down on me so disdainfully, or perhaps it's the gloom that makes me think so.'

He laughed. 'The upper landing then. Tell Foster to get it done. Did you see Lady Cunningham? How is she?'

'Not well, I'm afraid. She's fretting about Frederick, but there are signs she is beginning to condemn rather than forgive him. She's heard no word from him.'

'Is she planning to go to Greystones?'

'No. In fact, she is confined to her bed.'

'That's serious.'

'Just a wise precaution. She is breeding. It was apparently a complete reconciliation at Christmas. She has lost several babies before, and apart from wanting a son she loves children. Each loss has been a severe disappointment to her.'

'Yes, of course. Now, do you know the best modistes? The clothes that pretty Bavarian maid bought for you were all very well for the journey, but you need to buy plenty for the coming Season.'

Julia shrank inwardly. She knew how her marriage would seem to the *ton*. The Webbers, when they arrived, would be full of malicious gossip, and she had hoped for a respite, until other matters claimed their attention.

'I thought we were going to Courtlands?'

'We will, in a few days. But we are not going to give the gossips excuses to tear us to pieces, saying we are in hiding. Meanwhile, go and buy twice what you think you will need — '

'Twice?' Julia asked, laughing, then she gasped as she took the large roll of bills Sir Carey thrust into her hands.

'Or three times. Is this sufficient blunt? You've gone without for too long, and I intend to spoil you. Tomorrow or the next day we will drive in the Park, and see who is in Town yet.'

★ ★ ★

Julia could not bring herself to obey Sir Carey fully, and decided she would for the time being buy the minimum. She knew she had to look modish if she were to be a credit to him, and not invite sneers from people who despised her as a nobody and would consider him a credulous fool for marrying her. So she had to buy the best.

She needed help, for she did not know which modistes to go to, or what clothes she might reasonably be expected to need. The only person who might be of assistance was Elizabeth Pryce, so she hastily penned a note explaining her dilemma, and asking whether she could recommend places where she might go.

The reply came accompanied by Elizabeth Pryce herself. She waited in her barouche while Julia put on her pelisse, and they drove to Bond Street, where Elizabeth took charge.

Two hours later, the barouche laden with parcels, they returned to Upper Brook Street and handed Julia's purchases over to Molly while they retreated to the drawing-room and some reviving tea.

'I didn't know there were so many essentials,' Julia said. 'I thought a few gowns, and perhaps a shawl, along with what Sir Carey bought me in Bavaria, would be enough.'

'What we bought today will perhaps take you through a week or so of the full Season.'

'A week? Then I'd better find reasons for staying at Courtlands!'

'No, you must not,' Elizabeth said urgently.

'You must be seen, and behave as though there is nothing unusual or shameful in your situation. Your marriage was so unexpected, and from what you tell me Mrs Webber is likely to put it about that you trapped Sir Carey into it.'

'What? Surely not!'

'It's not unknown. Sir Carey will wish in any event to be in London so that he can hear what Napoleon is doing. If he leaves you down at Courtlands it will cause more gossip. So you must be here with him, and demonstrating it was a love match.'

Julia stared at her, aghast. How could she do that, pretend in front of the eager gaze of the *ton*, to something that was not true?

Elizabeth patted her arm. 'Don't look so frightened, child. It was obvious in Vienna that he was very taken with you, and many of the people who were there will have noticed it. Just behave naturally.'

'They'll think he married me on the rebound after Angelica jilted him,' Julia said.

'They'll think he had a fortunate escape from a chit who had her head turned last Season by all the admiration she was accorded. She must be ashamed, for I'm told she hasn't set foot in London since before Christmas. Now I must go back to your sister.'

*   *   *

Julia was toying with a roll at breakfast when Sir Carey, who had been out to visit some friends in the Horse Guards, came in carrying a copy of *The Times*. He pointed to the announcement of the marriage, privately in Bavaria, of Sir Carey Evelegh, Bt, and Miss Julia Marsh, daughter of the late Reverend and Mrs Marsh of Hampshire.

'So now we await the congratulations of our friends,' he said, smiling in a way that made her heart perform painful somersaults. 'Let us drive in the Park this afternoon, and some of them can meet us there. What had you planned to do today?'

'I thought I'd ask Mrs Carter to show me the house and explain to me how she has run it. I don't want to offend her again.'

'I think she is at least reconciled. She said to me how much brighter a few flowers made the house, just like it used to be in my mother's time. Then she apologized for not having thought of it herself, to welcome us home. Julia, the flowers in here seem to make the curtains look drab. Is it my imagination?'

Julia laughed. 'Not at all. They are so old, and Mrs Carter told me she dared not have them taken down to brush them in case they fell to pieces.'

'Then we must have new ones. And while we are about it, I suppose we should change the wallpaper too, or new curtains will make that look drab! Will you select whatever is needed, please, and it can be done while we are at Courtlands. I propose going there three days from now. Will that give you sufficient time?'

Julia blinked. 'You trust my taste?' she asked.

'Of course. My dear, I know that your sister bought you some clothes in Vienna, but I am sure you had the choosing of them, and they were in great good taste. As is that delightful gown you are wearing now. I take it you bought it yesterday?'

'Yes, and it was far more expensive than I thought reasonable, as there is so little material in it,' Julia said, glancing at the olive-green muslin morning dress Elizabeth had persuaded her she had to have, it suited her so well.

He grinned. 'It's irrelevant what it cost, if it suits you. I must get my mother's jewellery out of the bank for you to wear. But that reminds me, you have no betrothal ring, and only a cheap wedding band that pretty little maid from the inn bought for me. Come, let us go and see what Rundell and Bridge have.'

An hour later Julia possessed not only a

glittering gold wedding ring, but two more, one a huge solitaire diamond, the other a band set with emeralds, which had a matching necklace and bracelets.

'I feel like the beggar maid with King Cophetua,' she said, as they drove back home from Ludgate Hill.

He laughed. 'Trifles, and only what is due to my wife. When we have more time, and I know what colours you prefer for evening gowns, we will buy more.'

He helped her down from the phaeton and the groom led the horses round to the stables. Foster had the door open as they trod up the steps.

'Sir Carey, you have a visitor. Mr Daniel Fitzhugh.'

* * *

Sir Carey glanced ruefully at Julia. 'I didn't expect him to call quite so soon. He lives in Lincolnshire and isn't often in town, but he must have read the notice in *The Times*. I fear he may be a touch disappointed. When you've put off your hat come down to the drawing-room to meet Daniel.'

When Julia came down a few minutes later she could hear an angry voice before she opened the drawing-room door. She took a deep breath and went in.

The two men were standing one either side of the fireplace. Her first impression was that they were remarkably alike. Then she noticed small differences. Daniel, she presumed it was he, was a couple of inches shorter than Sir Carey and not so broad in the shoulder. His hair was thinner, and did not have the slight wave which made her want to run her fingers through it. His eyes were a paler blue, and set closer together. His nose was slightly crooked, his mouth thinner, and his ears stuck out. On his own, he might have been accounted tolerably handsome, but beside Sir Carey no one would call him that. His clothes were modish, but his cravat was intricately tied and his shirt points too high for comfort. He held a jewelled snuff box in his left hand, and as he looked at Julia he negligently flicked it open, and took a pinch, inhaling it as he stared insolently at her. So this was the man who was so obsessed with cats. She moved forward, her hand outstretched, determined to show him the civility he seemed disinclined to offer her.

'You must be my husband's cousin. I am so pleased to meet you, Mr Fitzhugh.'

It was with obvious reluctance that he took her hand, and he dropped it at once. 'So you're the chit he married,' he commented, giving her a disapproving look.

'Oh, thank you, sir! I've never been called a chit before, and it makes me feel younger than my age.'

Julia suppressed a smile. She sounded like a simpering ninny, and didn't dare look at Sir Carey for fear of bursting into laughter.

Daniel frowned. 'I thought he was betrothed to that Philpot gal.'

'Angelica decided she had made a mistake,' Sir Carey said, 'which was fortunate for me since it allowed me to offer for Julia. Now you have seen her, I am sure you will congratulate me on my good fortune,' he added sternly.

Julia dropped her gaze so that Daniel would not see the laughter in her eyes, for it was perfectly clear he had no wish to offer any congratulations, but remnants of politeness prevented him from saying so.

'When will you be going to Courtlands?' he asked instead. 'No doubt you'll be wishing to introduce your wife to your sisters. I gather they have not yet met her?'

'No. Julia and I met in Vienna. It was a whirlwind romance,' Sir Carey replied, and Julia now knew him well enough to detect amusement in his calm voice.

She glanced at him gratefully, for maintaining the pretence, while wishing it were true.

'I suppose she knew about your birthday

188

drawing near?' Daniel asked.

Julia decided it was time she joined in this odd conversation again. 'Indeed I do, Mr Fitzhugh,' she said brightly. 'I am hoping to organize some sort of celebration in July to mark it. Thirty is such a milestone, is it not?'

She thought she heard a slight choking sound from Sir Carey, but carefully avoided looking at him. Mr Fitzhugh frowned, snorted, and swung on his heel.

'I must take my leave, I'm already late for an appointment because you were out. But I take it ill in you not to inform your family of your intentions, instead of getting wed in that havey-cavey manner.'

He stalked out of the room, and Julia looked at Sir Carey, her eyes brimming with merriment.

'Oh dear, the cats will not get their usual attention tonight,' she said, and giggled. 'Is he always like that?'

'Most of the time. He cannot endure to be contradicted or worsted.'

'Then I'm not at all surprised his wife left him.'

★   ★   ★

On the following morning Sir Carey was waiting in a room at the Foreign Office to see

Lord Castlereagh, who had sent for him. He was smiling reminiscently at how baffled Daniel had looked to be confronted by Julia. Had he expected another Angelica?

It was odd, but he could scarcely recall what Angelica looked like. He retained a hazy impression of blonde curls and limpid blue eyes, but that was all.

Then his thoughts swung to the previous afternoon when he had driven Julia round the Park. She had looked charming in a pale-blue pelisse, with a neat matching hat. She had also looked calm, though when he handed her into the phaeton he'd felt her hands trembling in his.

The news of his marriage had spread rapidly, and they were hailed continuously by friends and acquaintances who wanted to meet the bride and congratulate him. Many expressed surprise at the haste, many complimented Julia, but none mentioned Angelica. It was as though she had never existed, and Sir Carey was beginning to look on that episode in his life as some sort of distant dream.

He'd seen admiration in the men's eyes, and known that the women were carefully assessing Julia's clothes, and speculating on why she had managed to snare him when so many of them, in the past, had not been able to.

The more serious wanted to ask questions about the Congress, and debate the prospects of a resumption of hostilities if Napoleon could once more gather together an army.

'Is Wellington going to take charge?' one elderly man asked. 'Why is he lingering in Vienna? Do you know, the two of them have never met in battle. That will be a clash of Titans, if it ever takes place.'

'I have heard no news from Vienna since Boney escaped from Elba,' Sir Carey told them. 'I think it might be premature to break off all the negotiations too soon, until we see what success he has in rousing the French once more. They have taken so long to come to some agreement, and we don't want to have to start all over again.'

'No, by gad! It's cost the Austrians a pretty penny, entertaining all those kings and hangers-on.'

Lord Castlereagh might have some news, but Sir Carey hoped he would not want to send him on some mission. He was eager to go home to Courtlands, not only to see the sisters he'd been away from for over six months, but to show his home to Julia. In some surprise, he realized that her opinion mattered to him. He'd liked her in Vienna, but appreciated her value during the past few weeks.

She had not complained once at the rigours of the journey. Comfortable as his travelling coach was, it was not ideal for four people trying to sleep as it was bounced over the icy ruts and the poor roads, made worse after the winter.

Already his London house seemed more like the home he remembered when his parents were alive. Could she work the same magic at Courtlands?

11

Fanny wished Julia was not leaving London. Courtlands was not a great distance, a day's journey, but in Vienna she had come to depend on her sister a great deal, and having been so recently reunited with her it seemed unfortunate she was going away again.

She was grateful to Elizabeth, of course she was, but she didn't feel able to talk about Frederick with quite the same freedom. After all, she and Mr Pryce scarcely knew him.

In the past she had accepted his dalliances with other women with resignation. So far as she could judge, most men had their flirts. Some men deserted their wives, but she was mortified at being of their number. To begin with she had wanted only that he would return to her, but as time went on and she heard nothing from him, she became worried. Where was he? Had they had an accident? Was he even dead? Surely, in such a case someone would have notified her.

She sent increasingly urgent messages to her butler at Greystones, asking if they had received any news, but the replies were always the same. Nothing had been heard. The children, at first, had asked almost every day when their father was coming home. Now, absorbed in the excitement of the journey and their new life with friends, they seemed to have forgotten about him. Perhaps, if he were dead, that was fortunate. They would not feel the loss so greatly.

How did she feel herself? She admitted privately that she was becoming angry rather than worried. If he did return, she thought with a sigh, she would probably accept him back. There was little else she could do, and despite it all she still loved him. She had nowhere to go. Her parents were dead, and they had few close relatives, no one closer than a second cousin, and he was an elderly bachelor who lived somewhere in the wilds of Devonshire and never came to London. She had only met him once, when she was about seven years old.

She roused herself from gloomy thoughts when Julia came into her room.

'I came to see how you are, and say goodbye for a while,' Julia said after she'd kissed Fanny.

'I'm much the same as always,' Fanny said. 'At least I haven't yet lost the child, and previously it was almost always before this stage.'

'So you must take extra care if it seems you

can carry this one,' Julia said bracingly.

Fanny nodded, wishing Julia's energy did not always make her feel weak and incompetent.

'You'll know how I feel when you're pregnant yourself,' she said. If Julia suffered from nausea and lassitude she might have more sympathy with her.

Julia was blushing slightly. 'Of course,' she said. 'We set off tomorrow, but I'm not sure how long we'll be staying at Courtlands. Sir Carey wants to be back in London fairly soon.'

'You'll meet his sisters. Does he have any other family?'

Julia laughed. 'A cousin, a most unpleasant man I had the misfortune to meet two days ago. He is, Sir Carey tells me, miserly in the extreme, spending only on a couple of dozen cats, and commissioning paintings and statues of the creatures. He was not pleased with our marriage.'

'Oh? Why not?'

Julia hesitated. 'I suppose he may have thought he would lose any inheritance. Apart from his sisters Sir Carey has no other heirs, so he might have expected to inherit something.'

'Well, you'd better hurry up and produce a couple of sons.'

Julia nodded, then said she had so much to do she really ought to be getting back to Upper Brook Street. 'Take care,' she said, and kissed Fanny. 'I'll come and see how you do, and whether you have heard anything, as soon as we are back in London.'

* * *

Julia breathed a sigh of relief as she went back home. She didn't want to keep secrets from Fanny, but she knew her sister would be likely to pass on anything she was told. It wasn't malice, simply that she did not think before speaking. If she knew the marriage was in name only, a business arrangement, she would not be able to refrain from speculating aloud about it. If she knew of the condition regarding Sir Carey's thirtieth birthday and his inheritance, she would instantly suspect the marriage had been arranged solely with that in mind.

Julia had wondered about it herself. It seemed odd that Sir Carey, who had apparently been much courted ever since he had graced the *ton*, should choose to marry Angelica, a girl so much younger than himself, just months before his birthday. From what he said, his attachment had not survived the long separation while he had been in Vienna, but he had swiftly provided himself with another wife, and without any pause to allow her a chance to reflect and refuse.

She had to thrust these speculations to the back of her mind when she reached home. Molly was fretting about which clothes to pack, and Julia, not knowing whether they would be entertaining at Courtlands, or visiting neighbouring families, decided she had better take everything.

'I don't have such a great deal,' she said.

'We'll need another trunk, though, if you take the clothes you had when you arrived.'

'I think they might be more suitable to the country than London, so yes, we'll take them. There must be some spare trunks somewhere. In the attics, I expect.'

'I'll ask Mrs Carter, and one of the footmen can bring it down.'

Julia left her to it, afraid she would begin to interfere. She had been so used to doing everything for herself it was difficult to remember she had people to do things for her. She went downstairs to the library. She'd been reading one of the new novels, *Waverley*, and wondering who the anonymous author was. She had just picked up the book when Sir Carey came into the room.

'Julia, how is Lady Cunningham? You were

planning to visit her, I believe?'

'She's fretful, but beginning to get angry with Frederick. I'm not sure if I want him to come home and discover he can't treat her so badly, or whether it might upset her so much she'll lose this child.'

'We'll be back in London soon, and you can support her. I understand Elizabeth Pryce is being a great help.'

'Yes. I don't know what we would have done without her. In all probability we'd still have been in Vienna, without any money, and only Frederick's dreadful grandmother to depend on. And if Napoleon recruits another army, we'd have had little chance of getting back to England. Is there any more news?'

'He's marching north, towards Paris. I believe the King is preparing to flee.'

'Giving up without fighting?' Julia asked, disbelieving.

'He probably suspects the citizens of Paris are not wholly with him.'

'The rest of the European powers won't want Napoleon restored. They are bound to mobilize against him.'

* * *

Sir Carey chose to drive his curricle, saying it was a fine day and Julia would appreciate the countryside better in an open carriage. His valet and Molly could follow with the luggage.

'You don't have much,' he teased Julia as they watched the trunks being loaded into the carriage the next morning.

'I have all my clothes,' she replied, startled.

'All? Then did you obey my instructions to purchase three times what you thought you needed?' he asked, as he helped her into the curricle and gave the horses the office to move.

'No, for that would have been far too much.'

He laughed. 'Please, Julia, accept that I am wealthy, I can well afford to clothe my wife in a fashionable manner. Or are gowns much more expensive than I thought? Did you spend all the money I gave you?'

'No,' Julia admitted, 'I will buy more later, when I am sure of what I need. But I can change the appearance of many of the gowns with different trimmings, and minor alterations,' she pointed out. 'I have been used to doing that in the past, and it's quite easy.'

'But it is not what you will be doing now. My wife will be a credit to me, with fashionable clothes. I think I had better accompany you on your next visit to the modistes.'

His tone was light, almost teasing, but Julia could hear the steel beneath the surface. Until now he had seemed mild, always calm, and she had a sudden realization that he could, if necessary, be implacable, even angry. She shivered. She would not wish to be the object of such anger.

He misunderstood. 'Are you cold? Do you want another rug?'

'No, thank you. Tell me about your sisters. I'm looking forward to meeting them.'

'Caroline is fifteen, an indefatigable letter writer. She will be sixteen in September and has been plaguing me for months to let her make her come out next year. But she is still a child, and sixteen is too young. I'd like to delay it until she is eighteen, but I doubt I'll be able to withstand her pleas. She won't sulk, that's never been her way, but she will mention it at every opportunity, telling me of all her friends who are going to be in London, and sighing that it would be so enjoyable to be there with them, and mortifying if she were left behind in the schoolroom while they were getting married.'

Julia laughed. 'Friends? Does she go to school? Is that where she made friends?'

'She has a good friend at the rectory, Penelope, who was also at the school. Last year there was some trouble. One of the older girls eloped with an infantry officer, a lad not much older than herself, who had been billeted in the town with his regiment. The school was not sufficiently vigilant. Caroline is a romantic, and I could not risk her following suit. I took the girls home and they have had a governess since then. Penelope is two years older and no longer needs one. But Caroline writes endlessly to all her other schoolfriends.'

'And her sister?'

'Susan is twelve, much quieter, utterly absorbed in music. She plays the pianoforte, violin and harp, and has been asking if she could learn to play the flute.'

'Goodness, she sounds talented. She was at the school too? Did they not mind leaving?'

'Caroline objected for a while, until she realized she could have far more freedom at Courtlands, to walk in the park or ride. Fortunately she likes her governess, Miss Trant, who is an excellent rider and can always accompany her. Susan much prefers it at home, for she can spend as much time as she likes on her instruments.'

He fell silent and Julia did not speak. She was enjoying the countryside, for they were driving through the Chiltern hills, and there was fresh new growth on the beech trees, and carpets of bluebells beneath them. There was a lot to think about. Would his sisters welcome her? And the rest of the household, would they accept her? Could she be the sort of wife Sir Carey wanted, or would he, one day, regret his impulsive marriage?

★ ★ ★

It was almost dusk when Sir Carey drove between some gateposts, and smiled as the woman who had opened them bobbed a curtsy.

'I will take you to see Mrs Saddler one day soon,' he said. 'If we stop now we will not reach the house before it's dark. Her tongue runs on forever.'

They were following a slightly curving drive, lined with chestnut trees which reminded Julia of the avenues in the Prater, and up a slight incline. When they breasted the summit and Sir Carey drew to a halt Julia gasped in delight.

'It's beautiful!' she breathed.

The house, built of golden stone, was in a slight hollow, and the low hills behind were framed by a glorious saffron and apricot and pale-green sunset. The long frontage, two storeys high, with many windows, had a central portico, and stood behind an ornamental lake. The drive swept round this, dividing so that one arm led to the back of the house. As Sir Carey drove on Julia's gaze was drawn upwards, and she could see beyond the house a square tower, of darker stone.

'Is that the castle?' she asked. 'But I thought castles were built on hilltops, so that they could see who was coming.'

'Not all. You can't see it from here, but the river is just beyond the house, and this castle must have been built to guard a crossing.'

'It's beautiful. And such a peaceful setting. I know I shall love it here.'

As she finished speaking the peace was broken as the front door opened, and what seemed like a whole pack of barking dogs erupted, followed by two girls who were frantically calling them to heel.

Sir Carey's grip on the reins tightened, and his tiger, muttering an oath, leapt down to run to the horses' heads. Between them they restrained the attempt to bolt, and within seconds two grooms arrived from the back of the house and held the bridles, persuading the horses to take the final few steps to the portico.

Sir Carey leapt down and held his hands up to Julia. Before she understood his intention, he grasped her by the waist and lifted her down.

'Welcome to Courtlands, my dear.' Then without raising his voice he commanded the dogs to lie down.

They obeyed instantly, but their tails continued to wag, and instead of barking they were giving excited, panting squeaks. Julia saw there were only three of them, a slender greyhound, a spaniel, and a terrier.

He turned to the girls, who were looking rather abashed. Both had dark, curly hair, and they were holding hands as though for mutual protection.

'We will discuss this later,' Sir Carey said sternly. Then his voice changed, became softer, and drawing Julia forward he said, 'Before then, you must meet your new sister, Julia.'

She had not been aware that he held his arm round her waist, and she felt herself grow warm from embarrassment.

'I'm so pleased to meet you,' she said. 'You must be Caroline? And Susan?'

They bobbed curtsys, both scrutinizing her eagerly.

'You're pretty,' the older one said. 'You're older than Angelica, but just as pretty in a different way. Carey wrote he was married, and we couldn't imagine what sort of girl he'd choose after her. It must have been so romantic, meeting in Vienna. I wonder if I will meet my husband in some romantic city like that, or just the usual way during the Season?'

'You won't be having your come out for ages and ages,' the younger girl said. 'Julia — may I call you that?'

'Of course,' Julia said, suppressing a smile. She quite saw what Sir Carey had meant when he said Caroline mentioned her come out at every opportunity.

'Thank you,' Susan said politely. 'Do you play the pianoforte? If you do, perhaps we could play duets? If you are good enough, that is. Miss Trant can play but she is so precise! She cannot improvise, or make up tunes like I can.'

'I hope you will find me adequate,' Julia said, struggling not to laugh. Were all girls their ages so plain-spoken?

Sir Carey, when she glanced at him, also seemed to be trying hard to suppress smiles. 'Come, let us go inside, and Julia can meet the rest of the household. Take those dogs round to the stables first.'

The girls grasped hold of the dogs' collars and dragged them, unwilling, away. Sir Carey, whose arm was still about her waist, turned towards the front door.

'I thought I had come to a household with a couple of dozen dogs instead of cats,' she murmured, and he laughed, and suddenly bent to kiss her briefly on the lips.

'Welcome,' he whispered, as he led her up the shallow flight of steps.

★ ★ ★

Julia watched Sir Carey, accompanied by three ecstatic dogs, ride away on the following morning. He needed, he said, to visit some of his tenants, but Julia might find the talk rather tedious. He would take her to meet them another day, when there would be time for proper introductions.

'So I suggest Caroline and Susan show you round the house.'

The girls were only too willing, and took Julia on an extended tour of the modern wings. The rooms were elegant, but the only rooms Julia felt were homelike were the schoolroom and the parlour which the girls and Miss Trant used. There, books and needlework and music sheets and painting materials were scattered in profusion.

Miss Trant was a tall, elegant woman in her thirties, and Julia took to her at once.

'Go and wait for Lady Evelegh downstairs,' she told the girls briskly. 'I wish to have a few words with her first.'

'You will ask?' Susan whispered loudly, and

Miss Trant smiled and nodded. Julia wondered in some amusement what it was Susan had not liked to mention herself.

'I've been in charge of these girls of necessity, while Sir Carey has been out of the country,' Miss Trant said bluntly. 'Now you are here, I hope you will tell me if there is anything you want me to do, or not to do.'

'I'm sure you are doing everything necessary,' Julia said, somewhat taken aback.

Miss Trant smiled. 'I hope so, but what I meant was that I shall not be offended if you have any suggestions or criticisms.'

'I really don't know enough about how to bring up girls of Caroline's and Susan's ages,' she confessed. 'I'm more likely to be coming to you for advice!'

'They are both very promising girls. Caroline needs to practise her French, for I am afraid she does not consider it a necessary accomplishment. I tell her that everyone with any pretence to education or culture speaks French, but she does not believe me. Perhaps you could mention how everyone in Vienna could converse in French even if they knew no English? Susan, however, has already outstripped me in her music. I think she would profit by having a specialist music teacher.'

'Do you know of anyone you could recommend?'

'My own old music teacher lives nearby, and though he does not take many pupils, he would take Susan if I asked him. My late father was the rector here,' she explained.

Julia had been told by Sir Carey that she was to supervise the education of his sisters. She took a deep breath. 'Then I think that is settled. Could we go and see him, take Susan?'

Miss Trant smiled. 'Good. Now I believe they want to show you the older part of the house.'

'The castle? I'm looking forward to that. Is any of it habitable?'

'They will show you what is safe, mainly what used to be the keep. The rest of it, the original gatehouse, is blocked off.'

Julia went down and found the girls in the kitchen, sitting at the table drinking cups of milk and eating freshly baked cakes. She smiled at the cook and took another chair. 'Those look delicious. May I have one?'

'And some milk, my lady? Fresh from the cow we keep for the household milk.'

All Sir Carey's servants seemed polite and friendly, by no means subservient, and she compared this to Fanny's household, where they had all trodden warily, afraid of offending Sir Frederick. After just a few hours she felt at home here.

The castle, or what remained of it, consisted of a three-storey keep and a few stretches of wall that had once enclosed the inner bailey. The gatehouse, fenced off, was on the far side of this old courtyard.

'We have to go in up these outer stairs,' Caroline explained. 'They always had the entrance on the first floor, so that it was easier to defend from invaders. This was the great hall. It's never used now, which I think is a pity. It would be wonderful to have meals here.'

'It's too far for the servants to carry the food,' Susan said. She seemed much more prosaic that Caroline, Julia thought, amused. 'It would be cold when it got here. Carey had new kitchens put in after our parents died, nearer the dining-room.'

'Well, it would be romantic,' Caroline insisted. 'There used to be rooms up here, but none of them has any furniture left,' she went on, leading the way up a narrow circular stair.

Julia looked into the small rooms on the next floor, and shuddered. She would hate to have lived in them, with the narrow slit windows that let in so little light. There were shadows and narrow passages which led, Susan told her, to the garderobes. 'The necessaries, you know,' she said, and giggled.

'Come on, let's go on the roof,' Caroline called, already halfway up the next spiral staircase. 'There's a lovely view of the river from up here.'

Julia stood beside the crenellated wall which ran round the edge of the tower, and the girls pointed out the church steeple visible over the trees bordering the drive, a lazily meandering river, and various farms she could see in the distance. 'That's Carey coming back,' Susan said, pointing. 'He owns all the land in this valley, and all the houses in the village. We'll take you round and introduce you one day soon, if Carey doesn't.'

They were delightful girls, Julia thought, as they went carefully down the stairs and out into the old bailey.

'What was the ground floor used for?' she asked.

'In the olden days, storage,' Caroline said. 'And to keep prisoners. I don't think there's anything there now. Let's see if the door will open.'

They walked along the side of the keep, past the massive buttresses, and stopped beside a relatively new door set into the wall. There did not appear to be any lock, so Caroline pushed it hard, and it moved a short way.

'Come on, let's all push together,' she said,

and Julia and Susan added their weight to hers.

Suddenly the door gave way, and as they toppled into the gloom beyond it Julia felt her skirt being pulled, as though someone were trying to pull her backwards, and at the same time heard a crashing noise just behind them. Clouds of dust blew up, and all three of them began to choke.

12

Sir Carey heard the screams as he left the stable yard, and began to run. The doors to the undercroft stood open, and all he could see was a large lump of stone and what appeared to be a body lying partly beneath it. Legs and feet were visible, and a strip of fabric which, through the cloud of dust that covered it, looked remarkably like the green gown Julia had worn that morning. His heart raced, and he found he was mouthing supplications to the Deity that she was still alive.

Someone was still screaming, someone else seemed to be sobbing, and then, with a surge of relief, he heard Julia speak.

'Caroline, dear, are you hurt?'

His sister replied, her words incoherent, but mercifully the screaming stopped.

He reached the doorway, saw his sisters cowering together a yard away inside the building, and knelt down beside Julia. 'Are you hurt?' he demanded. 'Julia, did it hit you?'

To his amazement she chuckled. 'No, not really. I think it scraped my leg, but I'm pinned here. I can't get up. The wretched thing's holding my skirt down.'

'We'll soon get you free.'

He stood up and began to heave the lump of rock away from her.

'Be careful! There may be other pieces coming down! If the wall up there's not safe, that one could have dislodged others.'

As she spoke she wriggled away from the stone, and her skirt tore on a jagged edge. But she rolled free, and Sir Carey spared a glance towards the battlements. Immediately above them he could just see a slight unevenness, where a portion of the wall had broken away. Then he turned his attention to Julia.

She was sitting composedly on the ground with the remnants of her skirt pulled round her legs, but one side of the skirt was slit and through it Sir Carey saw that the skin on her lower leg had been scraped raw.

'Let me look,' he demanded. 'No, don't pull away from me, I won't hurt you. Caroline, are you hurt? Or Susan?'

'No, we — we were further inside than Julia,' Caroline said.

Sir Carey was carefully feeling Julia's leg, and ignoring her protests that she was only slightly hurt, and quite capable of dealing with it herself.

'Good. Susan, you can stop crying, I need your help. Go and find Molly, and ask her to take water and salves to Julia's room. Caroline, go and find a cloak or something Julia can wear over this dress. It's ruined, and I don't suppose she wants to walk through the house in such a state.'

'You can let me speak for myself,' Julia interrupted, struggling away from him. 'I can walk, and as everyone will soon know what happened, I don't need to cover my shame!' She laughed shakily. 'I'd like the water and salves, but if Caroline comes back with me she can call for help if I swoon from the excitement. I'd prefer you to go up and see why that rock fell. It all seemed quite firm when we were up there a few minutes ago, and there's no wind. What made it fall?'

He looked at her and nodded. He'd been so concerned with making sure she was not badly hurt he hadn't given a thought to how the stone had fallen.

'I'll come and see you as soon as I've looked.'

★   ★   ★

Julia breathed a sigh of relief as she set off back to the house, with Caroline solicitously holding her arm. His touch on her leg had sent shivers coursing through her veins. It was similar to the sensations she had felt when, after the wedding, he had kissed her. Every time he touched her, to hand her from a carriage, or to guide her into a room, she seemed to tremble, but fortunately he did not appear to notice this. Briskly, she turned her thoughts away from him.

'Caroline, it looks as though the top of the keep isn't safe, but we kept away from the battlements. Did you see anything odd up there?'

'No, but I wasn't looking at them, I was showing you the view. Are you sure you're not badly hurt?'

'I'll no doubt have a massive bruise, and it feels sore, but I was fortunate. It could have broken my leg, or worse. It was lucky you and Susan were right inside, and I almost was.'

'Carey will forbid anyone to go near the castle now,' Caroline said.

'Then it's fortunate I was able to see it first.'

They were silent while making for a side door, and going up the back stairs to Julia's room. None of the servants saw them, and though Julia had made light of it to Sir Carey, she was relieved not to have them see her in such a filthy and dishevelled state.

'Go and find Susan, and both of you

change your gowns,' Julia suggested. 'The dust seems to have covered you as well as me.'

'But I want to help you.'

'Molly can do all I need. You ought to go and make sure Susan is all right. Find something to do to distract her thoughts.'

Caroline pouted, but went when she saw that Molly was waiting for Julia. After her first exclamations of dismay, Molly set to and helped Julia take off her ruined gown, then gently bathed the leg and smoothed on a salve.

'It's got a mixture of comfrey and woundwort,' she said. 'It'll soothe it. And I'll get some crushed parsley to ease the bruising later. Cook said to drink this tisane, it will ease your nerves and you'll be able to sleep for a while.'

Julia was about to reply that her nerves didn't need soothing, and she didn't want to sleep, but everyone was being so solicitous it would be churlish to refuse. Suddenly the soft goose-feather mattress seemed desirable, so she made no protest when Molly produced her nightgown, and allowed herself to be tucked up without protest.

★ ★ ★

Sir Carey considered the space on the battlements where the fallen stone had rested. The stone below was slightly hollowed at the top, and much paler than the exposed stones around it. Even a strong wind would have been unlikely to move it. And there had been no wind. He peered more closely, and soon spotted some scratches which seemed newly made in the join of the next two stones along. It looked suspiciously like an attempt to prise away the top stone with a knife or some other such tool. On even closer inspection of the gap there were a few marks which could have been made in the same way.

This indicated human intervention, and he felt a sudden surge of fury at the thought that his womenfolk had been in danger. Had it been an accident, some idiot fooling around and trying to see whether the stones were loose, or had it been a deliberate attempt to injure, or even kill, Julia? Or, he belatedly recalled, one of his sisters?

Thoughtfully he went back down the spiral stairs and through to the walled garden where he knew his head gardener was currently occupied. After a few general remarks he casually asked whether the man was satisfied with his under gardeners. 'I suppose you know what they are up to, all the time?' he said.

'That I do, sir,' was the reply. 'I sets 'em tasks, and know how long it should take 'em, so woe betide any as I find idling.'

'The pot boy, he's new, isn't he? Is he a hard worker? I know some lads that age can still be children, playing about when they think no one's watching.'

'Young Harry's me sister's lad, and though he's but ten he knows better than to take liberties.'

Next Sir Carey went to the stables, where the head groom was sitting in the sunshine polishing a bridle. The same casual questions elicited the information that one of the grooms had gone down to the village on an errand, and the other was exercising the mare he'd chosen and sent down from London for the new Lady Evelegh to ride.

'Not knowing how handy her ladyship is, sir, I thought it best to take the edge off the mare's spirits. Will you be riding out again today?'

'Not today. Tomorrow, perhaps.'

He strolled away, his thoughts in a whirl. If, and it seemed most likely, this was a deliberate attempt on Julia's life, would any of his servants have been involved? He could scarcely question every one of them. Most of them had worked for him for years, many of them for his father too. It would have been possible for a stranger to enter the grounds and find his way unseen to the top of the keep, but how could anyone have known Julia would be there just at that moment? Could it have been one of the village lads, curious about the castle, simply messing about with a new knife, as he'd been known to do himself, with unintended consequences? An accident rather than a premeditated attack?

It was impossible to tell. If it had been some lad he would have been terrified of discovery, and would have escaped back to the village as soon as possible. Sir Carey came to the conclusion that was what had happened. There was nothing to be done, apart from having the stairs to the top of the keep blocked off to prevent another such accident.

He made his way more briskly to the estate carpenter's shed, where he knew the man was mending some kitchen chairs, and gave his orders. 'Some of the stones on the battlements are loose,' he explained. 'I don't want any more being dislodged and falling down.'

That, he decided, would be the explanation. There was no point in revealing what he knew and starting yet more gossip and speculation in the house and village.

★   ★   ★

When Sir Carey got back to the house he found Julia asleep. He stood beside the bed looking down at her. It was the first time he'd seen her asleep, apart from in the travelling coach, and he felt a sudden rush of tenderness, seeing her so vulnerable, and knowing he had so nearly lost her. Her mouth turned down slightly at the corners, whereas normally it was cheerfully smiling, and he wondered if she was having terrifying dreams. She had been so calm at the castle, soothing his sisters, who had not been so close to disaster, but he knew how one could, later, relive frightening events which had happened so fast there had not been leisure to panic or be worried at the time.

Unable to settle to anything, he wandered round the house. Having seen the difference Julia's slight changes at the London house had made, he now noticed things he had before taken little heed of. The rooms, though scrupulously cleaned by his servants, looked cold and uninviting. There were no flowers. In the drawing-room the chairs were ranged in rigid rows against the walls. The pictures were dark and gloomy, and any ornaments displayed were placed with no attention to order or compatibility.

Had it been like this in his mother's day? It was a long time ago, and he recognized, somewhat ruefully, that small boys tended neither to notice nor care about their surroundings. He'd been much older during his father's second marriage, but most of the time he'd been away at school or Oxford or in the army. During many vacations he had visited the homes of friends, or gone on walking or reading holidays with them. Since the second Lady Evelegh had died her daughters had been at school or in the charge of governesses, and for a while he had been in Russia. No one would have wanted to make changes in case they had offended him. Briefly he wondered whether Julia, if she had been a governess in a like situation, would have dared.

Miss Trant, though efficient and pleasant, and a prime favourite with the girls, would not have presumed. Though she had known the family all her life, she was a stickler for formality, still the daughter of a rector who had depended for his living on the Eveleghs.

Still restless, he went back to the castle keep to see what progress the carpenter had made in blocking off the stairs. The man was making a good job of it. There were some stout bars held in place by brackets fixed to the walls. Anyone wishing to get past them would need an axe or a set of tools. He complimented the man and wandered back to the house, to find his steward waiting for him. He was able to immerse himself in estate matters until it was time for dinner, and when he went into the drawing-room it was to find Julia there, directing one of the footmen where to place huge bowls of flowers.

The chairs had been moved, too. Some were drawn up before a cheerfully blazing fire, others arranged in small groups just right for conversations. Julia looked up and smiled at him.

'My dear, should you be out of bed?'

'I'm perfectly all right, sir, apart from a bruise on my leg. Even that does not pain much, thanks to the salve your housekeeper provided. It's better than any I've had before, and I must ask her for the receipt.'

★   ★   ★

On the following morning Julia insisted she was quite able to ride. 'I am longing for some exercise,' she told Sir Carey, 'and wish to meet some of your people as soon as possible. At least let us go to the home farm, and the lady who keeps the gates. I promise I will tell you if I am tired or in discomfort.'

She accompanied him to the stables, saying she wished to see where her new mare was housed. 'As well as speak to the groom who looks after her.'

Samuel, he said his name was, and came from near York.

'You're a long way from home,' Julia commented.

'Aye, but I've kinsfolk living near, and none of me own left back in Yorkshire. May as well bide here.'

'Well, the mare looks healthy, and well turned out,' Julia said, and took the reins while she spoke softly to the mare, who nuzzled at her shoulder. She was a finely-boned roan, with two white socks on her forelegs, and bright intelligent eyes. Julia knew she would enjoy riding her.

'I rode Daisy yesterday, me lady, she's shaken off the fidgets. Ye'll find her a steady ride.'

Julia smiled to herself. When her parents were alive she'd often ridden the horses belonging to the local squire, for she'd been the same age as his daughter, and they had roamed the countryside together. Most of those horses had been strong hunters, but she was a natural horsewoman and had easily controlled them.

She led Daisy over to the mounting block and was up in the saddle before Samuel or Sir Carey could help her. She stifled a twinge as her bruised leg rubbed against the pommel, but soon found a comfortable position.

Sir Carey mounted a large black gelding, a new hunter he intended taking to the hunting box in Leicestershire if it proved capable of tackling the country there. 'If not, there are several hunts we could join in these counties. You would like to hunt?'

'Indeed I would. It's been a few years since I was able to, as being companion to an elderly lady didn't include accompanying her on horseback, let alone hunting.'

'We'll leave the dogs at home today,' Sir Carey said, and told Samuel to take the disappointed trio back to the house. 'They might upset Daisy until she's used to them.'

They soon reached the home farm, a neat thatched house with a large yard surrounded by barns and sheds. A flock of hens scuttled away as they rode in, and two dogs which had been sleeping in the weak sunlight woke up and came towards them, barking.

Daisy shied, but Julia was able to control her, as a woman appeared at the farmhouse door and called the dogs to heel.

'My lord, I didn't hear you coming. I'm that sorry about the dogs. My lady, are you all right?'

Julia nodded, and glanced at Sir Carey. The black gelding had taken fright, and was doing his best to bolt, but Sir Carey was in control, and soon the horse settled down.

'Mrs Harris, good day to you. I came to see how you do, and introduce my wife.'

'And glad we all are to see you wed, sir. Will ye both come inside and have some ale and perhaps one of my scones? I baked them fresh this morning.'

By this time a gangling lad of about fifteen had emerged from one of the barns and come to hold the horses. Sir Carey slid from the saddle and came to lift Julia down.

'That would be very welcome,' Julia said, holding her hand out to Mrs Harris.

Mrs Harris bobbed a curtsy, then shyly took Julia's hand for a moment. 'It's glad we all are to see Sir Carey wed at last,' she said again. 'We want little ones up at the manor, that we do, and at times we thought we'd never get any. But ye looks a healthy enough lass. Jed, go and fetch your pa, he's in the five acre. Come in, do, and please excuse the state of the kitchen. Baking day, it is.'

'Everything smells delicious,' Julia said, ushered in front of Mrs Harris into a large, cheerful kitchen. On the table, cooling, were trays of scones, a large fruit cake, several loaves of bread, and half-a-dozen pies.

'You keep a good table,' Julia said, relishing the aromas.

'That I do, wi' Mr Harris and eight growing lads and lasses to feed! Now sit down, do. Or would you prefer the parlour? But there's no fire lit there.'

'This is wonderful,' Julia reassured her, and pulling out a stool sat at the big table. 'I much prefer kitchens when they're as welcoming as this one.'

Mrs Harris fetched a large cheese, some butter and a jar of strawberry jam from the pantry, set plates and knives in front of Julia and Sir Carey, who had pulled out another stool opposite, and began to carve one of the loaves.

We won't need to eat again today, Julia thought in amusement, and wondered how they might avoid having to eat half of the good things on the table.

Fortunately Sir Carey was used to Mrs Harris and her overwhelming hospitality. He held up his hand and laughed. 'Mrs Harris, I'd love just a slice of that bread and a hunk of cheese, and I'm sure Julia would too, but that's enough, really it is, or Cook will threaten to leave when we can't eat her dinner.'

'And a scone? Ye can wrap them up in a clean napkin to take with you. You won't be offered such fare at any of the other farms,' she added.

'We haven't time to visit any more of the farms today,' Sir Carey replied, and Julia approved his diplomacy. She was certain every housewife where they called would be only too anxious to display her own cooking skills. It would not do to be comparing them.

'What's this we hear of an accident yesterday?' Mrs Harris asked after a few moments. 'My lady here was almost killed, they said.'

'A stone fell from the roof of the old keep,' Julia told her. 'It was so ridiculous, it pinned my skirt to the ground and I couldn't get up until Sir Carey came and rolled it away. It must have been loose. Maybe when we pushed open the door of the undercroft, which the girls were anxious to show me, it was dislodged.'

'It would take a dratted great push to rattle they thick old walls,' Mrs Harris said.

'You know the old part of the manor hasn't been used for years,' Sir Carey said. 'No one has checked recently if the battlements are safe. But that stair is blocked off now, no one can get up on to the roof. So I don't want the village lads trying, out of curiosity.'

She gave him a hard look, but said no more. Just then Mr Harris came in and the talk turned to farming matters, last year's harvest, the health of the animals, and what he was planting this season.

Soon afterwards they rose to leave. Sir Carey lifted Julia into the saddle and felt her wince.

'Your leg, it hurts?'

'Just a twinge, on contact with the pommel. It's much better today.'

'All the same, we'll go home now. You've done enough.'

★   ★   ★

Though she contrived to behave as normal Julia was thankful when she was able to retire to bed. Her leg was throbbing, and the exertion of riding had been more of an effort than she had admitted. When Molly came to draw her curtains on the following morning and suggested she might like breakfast in bed, Julia happily agreed.

'His lordship said to tell you he's gone to visit more farms today, my lady. He won't be back till dinner-time. He hopes you will rest.'

'And not go exploring more ruined castles,' Julia interpreted, and laughed. 'Do the girls have lessons today?'

'Yes, Miss Trant gave them a holiday to greet you, but they'll be free this afternoon, and may want to go for a gentle walk, to show you the gardens.'

'That sounds safe enough,' Julia said, wondering whether Sir Carey had issued these instructions for her entertainment.

She spent a quiet morning strolling round the house, noting things she wanted to change. The curtains here were in even worse condition than at the London house, and she determined to measure how much fabric was wanted and visit one of the warehouses when she was next in London. She fetched her watercolours and crayons, and tried to match the shades of the wallpapers in the different rooms. Some of these were old, but particularly beautiful. The one in the dining-room was Chinese, she was certain, and probably valuable. That could be cleaned, if done carefully.

The girls and Miss Trant appeared and joined her for a meal of ham and fruit. Then Miss Trant asked if she was wanted, for if not she would retire and write some letters.

Julia and the girls fetched wraps, for the wind was cold, and went out into the garden.

'Sir Carey tells me you write many letters, Caroline.'

'Oh yes, I do, to all my schoolfriends.'

'And relatives?'

'My mother's sisters, and some cousins, but there are no other Eveleghs, or relatives on Papa's side apart from Cousin Daniel.

He's an unpleasant person, who would not reply in any case. So I never write to him. I'm so glad Carey married you after Angelica jilted him. I was afraid Cousin Daniel would get Carey's grandfather's money, and that would have been a great shame. Did you know he was at the same house party in Yorkshire as Angelica at Christmas? She wrote to say he was there.'

'You correspond with Angelica?' Julia said, surprised.

'Yes. She was at school with us, though she was two years older than me. She was the same age as Penelope. She's the rector's daughter, and she was there too. She doesn't write many letters, though. She didn't write to say she was going to marry someone else instead of Carey. It was Phoebe Norton, who was also there, who told me, but I haven't heard any more from her either. Julia, will you ask Carey if I can have my come out next year? I'll be sixteen, and Angelica was only a little older when she came out, and became engaged to Carey.'

'That will be for your brother to decide. But you don't have to hurry into a Season and a betrothal yet. You have plenty of time. Girls your age don't usually know what they want. Angelica didn't, did she?'

13

Two days later Julia again accompanied Sir Carey on farm visits. This time they went in the opposite direction, to an outlying farm at the end of the valley where Courtlands lay. This was more rugged country, the beginning of the Cotswold hills, and Julia saw several flocks of sheep. Because of this, they had again left the dogs at home.

'I cannot trust them not to chase the silly things,' Sir Carey explained, laughing. 'If the sheep turned and faced them the dogs would run away, as they do when they encounter the stable cat.'

Julia's leg had been stiff, and he must have noticed her slight wince when she mounted Daisy, for he did not take the direct route over hedges and walls which had been their previous mode of riding, but led the way decorously through gaps in the walls or gateways in the hedges. Julia had to blink away a sudden wetness in her eyes when she realized his silent consideration for her. She had been attracted to him in Vienna, incredulous and barely able to credit her good fortune when they were married, but she wondered whether she could endure spending the rest of her life with him in this polite friendship. Feeling guilty for even admitting such thoughts to herself, she knew she wanted more, to be a true wife, and to bear his children.

Would he ever turn to her? Once, long ago, when she had been a child and had not understood, her mother had spoken disparagingly about one of the local gentry, saying that some men had uncontrollable carnal appetites, but she wished he would indulge them away from home, rather than inflict them on helpless maidservants. Their own dairy maid had suddenly left the village, and later Julia had overheard another village girl saying what a shame it was she couldn't keep her baby.

Years later these events had come together and made sense to the older Julia. Now she wondered, rather desolately, whether Sir Carey would satisfy his sexual appetites elsewhere. He was young and vigorous, surely he had normal desires. He'd married her in haste, perhaps without thought, promising her he would not ask from her the normal married duties. He was honourable, she knew, and would keep that promise, but she was beginning to wish he had not made it, and consider ways in which she might encourage him to forget it.

As they reached the farm Julia's mood of despondency had lifted, and she was smiling to herself as she envisaged scenes of seduction in which she enticed Sir Carey into her bed. Should she, when they returned to London, equip herself with some of the outrageously indelicate nightgowns she had seen? Shocked though she had been at the time, she had later admitted to herself she would like to wear them, for her own satisfaction as well as their apparent power over susceptible husbands.

'You look happy,' Sir Carey commented, as he swung down from his horse and came across to lift her from the mare.

'It's a lovely day,' Julia said, feeling herself go hot with embarrassment at her lascivious thoughts. She trembled as his hands gripped her waist and she swung her leg over the pommel. As he lowered her to the ground she held on to the pommel to steady herself, and then exclaimed in dismay as the whole saddle slid towards her. They both stepped backwards and the saddle fell to the ground.

As they stared at it one of the farmer's sons, a brawny lad of sixteen, ran out of the cowshed and took the reins from Sir Carey, who bent down to examine the saddle.

'The devil!' Sir Carey exploded.

'The girths be broke,' the lad said.

'Sir Carey, what's amiss?'

The farmer's wife had appeared from the kitchen, looking anxious. 'Ben, what have 'ee done?'

'He's done nothing,' Sir Carey said, his voice grim. 'Mrs Smith, may I bring this into your kitchen to have a closer look at it?'

'To be sure, sir. And this must be Lady Evelegh. Welcome, ma'am, to Hill Farm. Come in, both of ye, and I'll find some bread and cheese. Ben, when ye've tethered the horses, go and fetch me some cider.'

Sir Carey took Julia's arm and led her inside the low-beamed kitchen. It was similar to the others she had seen, bright and cheerful with a warm range on which stood various pots, and on the huge scrubbed pine table plenty of evidence of baking in progress.

They sat down, and Sir Carey turned up the saddle. 'See here,' he said, holding up the end of the girth strap. 'This has been cut through, almost to the end.'

'It hasn't just frayed?' Julia asked, leaning across and fingering the webbing strap.

'No, the cut's clean, done with a knife. And it was hidden by the saddle flap. This was deliberate. My God, if we'd been taking jumps as normal, and it had broken, you'd have taken a nasty fall!'

'Wicked,' Mrs Smith said, peering over Sir Carey's shoulder. 'Ye could have broken your neck, me lady, if ye'd fallen on they walls.'

Sir Carey took a deep breath. 'That new groom! I'll see to it he never works in a stables again!'

As Mrs Smith pressed food and cider on them, he frowned in thought. It hadn't been carelessness. Who could have wanted to injure, perhaps kill Julia? He glanced up at her, and wondered at her apparent calm. She was pale, and there was an anxious look in her eyes. She must have reached the same conclusion as he had, that someone wanted to hurt her, but she was smiling at Mrs Smith and asking about her family, nodding as the farmer's wife went into copious detail about all the childish ills the younger ones had suffered this past winter.

'Can we borrow a girth strap?' he asked when Mrs Smith paused for breath. 'Julia can't ride home on this saddle as it is.'

'To be sure ye may. Ben'll find ye one.'

'Or would you prefer to wait here while I fetch a carriage?' he asked Julia, suddenly aware she might not wish to ride so soon after such a shock.

She shook her head. 'I will ride, and in future I'll check everything first,' she said, but her smile was tremulous.

'And so will I. Which tells me I ought to go and check the bridles and my own saddle,' he said. 'Will you excuse me?'

In the barn where Ben had tethered the horses and given them nets of hay to munch on, he found the boy already looking over the bridles.

'Your saddle's not been touched,' Ben said, 'but look-ee at this.'

He proffered the small bridle, and showed how the stitching on one rein near one of the rings had been broken, so that only a couple of threads held the leather together.

Sir Carey went cold. Whoever had done this had intended to make sure. It was only thanks to the careful, gentle way they had made this ride that both rein and girth strap had held as long as they had.

Ben assured him the rest of the gear was in good shape, but he went over everything himself, while Ben went off to find a needle and some strong thread, saying he was used to mending the harnesses of their own horses.

Ben also found a girth strap, and Sir Carey made sure it was fixed properly. They would ride back at a walk, and he would be alongside Julia all the way, ready to catch her should anything more happen, or should she faint. She had shown remarkable fortitude so far, but in his experience females often succumbed to the vapours once the initial shock had lessened. They put it down to greater sensibility than men possessed.

Angelica, he thought suddenly, would probably have swooned. It was the first time he had permitted himself to think of Angelica since the initial hurt and anger at her defection had cooled, and he swiftly banished the image of her from his mind. It was done, she was lost for him, and there was no profit in even thinking about what might have been. She was out of his reach, and he was married to Julia.

Then he grinned. Somehow he didn't think Julia was quite so feeble as to let herself react to shocks in such a manner. She had considered his outrageous proposal of marriage calmly, had judged his arguments in favour, and as calmly accepted. He wondered at himself. Had he been mad? Had the knock on the head which had felled him the night before addled his wits? He'd behaved in a manner quite alien to his normal common sense, but it had seemed sensible at the time. She was making his homes more comfortable and attractive, his sisters and the servants all seemed to like her, and his tenants showed their approval. The bargain they had made was proving to be satisfactory, and in addition he had thwarted his cousin's ambitions, which might be an ignoble thought but was a satisfying one.

★ ★ ★

When they reached Courtlands the head groom came to take the horses.

'Where is Samuel?' Sir Carey asked, and Julia thought she had never before heard him quite so furiously and coldly angry.

'I don't know, sir. He left soon after you rode away yourself. He slipped off, no one saw him go, but he's taken his belongings. Didn't even wait for the wages he was due.'

'I'll warrant he didn't!'

Sir Carey turned away and lifted Julia down from the mare. 'Go inside and rest, my dear, I'll explain.'

Julia nodded without speaking and went up to her room. Thankfully, she saw no one, and didn't bother to ring for Molly to help her out of her riding habit. When she had replaced it with a simple morning dress she sat down on the window seat and tried to order her thoughts. The accident of the falling stone might, now, be considered no accident. It could have been a deliberate attempt to kill her. This latest discovery could not have been anything other than deliberate. She could merely have suffered a bad fall, but it was equally possible she could have broken her neck. Samuel, by his disappearance, seemed to have admitted his guilt. Had he also been responsible for the falling stone?

Who might want her dead? Her marriage had directly affected Sir Carey's cousin by depriving him of their grandfather's legacy, but she and Sir Carey were legally wed. Surely, even if she died, this would not invalidate the inheritance? Her knowledge of the law was hazy, but logic would suggest that once the conditions for inheriting had been in place, they could not be overturned. She recalled Sir Carey telling her cousin Daniel's own wife had deserted him soon after their marriage, so he would have been in the same position as Sir Carey, wifeless. Yet she presumed he was still married, so that might make a difference. It didn't make sense. What could Daniel achieve by harming her? It could only be revenge.

Had Daniel employed Samuel for that? The man had come, he said, from Yorkshire. Daniel lived in nearby Lincolnshire, so the man might have been his own servant. How long had Samuel been employed at Court-lands? She didn't know, but for her own peace of mind she would find out. If he had arrived after their marriage had been announced, it would prove her suspicions.

She consoled herself with the thought that he had gone now. He was in no position to try to harm her again. The thought brought some comfort, and when Sir Carey knocked softly at the door she welcomed him with a bright smile.

'Sir Carey, come in. I've been trying to make sense of it all.'

'As I have. How do you feel? Should you not be in bed, resting?'

Julia laughed. 'I'm not a delicate flower. Yes, it was a shock, but no more. I cannot stop wondering what it's all for.'

'And your conclusions?'

'I don't want to accuse your cousin,' she said slowly, 'but he is the only explanation I can think of.'

She explained her reasoning, and he, it appeared, had been thinking along the same lines.

'The man Samuel came here a few days after the announcement of our wedding. One of the young grooms had left rather suddenly, with some incoherent story of a sick relative in Devon, and Samuel providentially appeared the following morning. As they were concerned not to be short handed when I came home, they accepted him on a month's trial. I presume the other groom had been paid well to leave.'

$$\star \quad \star \quad \star$$

When she did not ride out with Sir Carey, Julia spent the afternoons rambling about the gardens and the home park with his sisters. Caroline was a great talker, and only too eager to relate everything she knew about her brother. Both she and Susan clearly adored him.

'Except that he won't agree to my having my come out next year,' Caroline complained when Julia commented on this.

Julia laughed. Caroline was very persistent, and she heard this complaint almost every day. 'You are very young,' she said. 'You would really enjoy it all the more when you are a year older. Do you go to the Assemblies locally?'

'Not yet, but Carey has promised to take me soon. Julia, you could persuade him; you're his wife, and from what people say, new wives can persuade their husbands to do anything! Julia,' she added more slowly, 'what is marriage really like?'

I wish I knew, Julia thought wistfully, for her marriage was not a normal one. Before she could find an acceptable way of answering Caroline's question, Susan interrupted them.

'Look,' she said, pointing, 'there are some

of the village boys down by the river. Are they fishing?'

'Carey allows them to,' Caroline said. 'Let's go and see who they are. The bigger one looks like the rector's son. I expect he's home from Harrow.'

The boys both turned out to be sons of the rector. Julia had seen them at the village church on Sunday, but they had not been introduced. There had been so many people who wanted to greet Sir Carey and his new wife, the rector had shooed them away. They stood up and eyed Julia with interest when Caroline, assuming the air of a grand lady, introduced them.

'Have you caught much?' Julia asked. 'I used to love tickling trout when I was a girl.'

'They aren't being co-operative today, my lady,' the older boy, Robert, said. 'We did better the other day.'

Peter broke in. 'Is that roan mare yours?' he demanded. 'The one with two white socks? I saw her before.'

'When did you see her?'

'Last Wednesday, when we were here. She was tied up in that clump of trees near the old castle.'

'It was Thursday,' Robert contradicted.

'Wednesday.'

'Thursday. We had the trout for supper.'

Julia looked across at the square keep. The steps up to the entrance were visible. Thursday was the day of the accident there. This must have been the first attempt on her life. Julia was now convinced the falling rock had been deliberate. Samuel had been out, ostensibly exercising the mare, but if he had left her, so close to the castle, he could easily have seen them going into it and followed, to take that sudden opportunity.

She shivered, and Caroline asked if she were cold.

'A little. The sun's gone in, and there's a heavy cloud coming. I think we'd best go back to the house. Good luck with your fishing, boys.'

★　★　★

That evening, after dinner, Sir Carey and Julia sat in the library, a room both preferred to the more formal drawing-room. Susan was playing on the parlour pianoforte, and Caroline, who had a good singing voice, was with her, practising a new song.

When Julia reported what the boys had said Sir Carey agreed this proved Samuel's guilt. 'I've done what I can to trace him. The constable is making enquiries in the villages round about, but so far no one knows anything. What Samuel said about relatives in the district was clearly a lie. Apparently he didn't frequent any of the taverns, so none of the men other than the servants here knew much about him. That in itself seems unusual. I've never before known a groom who didn't enjoy himself at an inn when work was done.'

'I doubt we'll ever find him. He must be many miles away now.'

'I'm having enquiries made in the villages round about too. I could ask for a Bow Street Runner, but the man seems to have left no trace. I'm sending a man who knows him to Lincolnshire. If he's a tool of Daniel's, perhaps he will return there, to report his failure.'

'He left before he could have known the last attempt failed,' Julia pointed out. 'He hadn't been seen in the village that day, so how would he discover what happened? None of the other servants is likely to have had any contact with him.'

'I imagine the news of your death or injury would have been known all over the county within a day or so,' Sir Carey said. 'He could have lingered a few miles away and listened to the gossip where he wouldn't be known.'

On the following morning he was closeted in the estate room with his steward, when there was a sudden commotion in the hallway. A girl's shrill voice was demanding to see Sir Carey immediately.

'You will be sorry if you don't tell me where he is,' she said, and burst into tears.

'What the devil?' Sir Carey leapt to his feet and almost ran from the room. Julia was emerging from the morning-room where she had been making lists of what she would need to buy when they went back to London. Standing in the centre of the entrance hall, gesticulating with her riding whip to keep a bemused footman well away from her, was an enchantingly pretty girl. She was petite and slender, and the sapphire-blue riding habit enhanced her blonde loveliness and perfectly matched her eyes, made more brilliant by the tears which filled them.

She turned when she heard Sir Carey's footsteps, and ran across the hall to throw herself into his arms. Short of letting her fall to the floor Sir Carey had no option but to catch her. He tried to set her down, but she wound her arms round his neck and clung to him, bursting into a renewed bout of sobbing.

'Carey! Carey, my dearest love! Why didn't you wait for me?' she asked, her voice tremulous.

'Let us all go into the library,' Julia broke in. 'Ask Molly to bring some smelling salts and laudanum,' she ordered the footman, who scuttled away with less than his normal dignity.

Sir Carey carried the clinging damsel into the library, where she consented at last to release him and collapse into one of the deepest armchairs.

'What on earth are you doing here, Angelica?'

'I came to see you, of course!' she replied, and burst into a renewed bout of weeping.

Sir Carey cast a harassed look at Julia, who was standing calmly near the door.

'You rode here alone?'

'Yes, of course! If I'd ordered the carriage Mama would have forbidden it. But I had to see you! Why did you marry her?'

She threw a venomous glance at Julia, who returned the look impassively.

'This is my wife,' Sir Carey said. 'Julia, this is Angelica. I am afraid I cannot furnish you with her real name, since I never heard who she married.'

Angelica swallowed her sobs. She turned her face up to him, and Sir Carey saw with a shock that she could, unlike most girls, cry without her eyes reddening. She had never cried before, in his presence, and though he had been accustomed to the childish tantrums of Caroline and Susan in the past, this was different. She looked as lovely as he remembered, even in her obvious distress.

Molly came in at that moment with smelling salts and a small glass bottle of laudanum. She looked curiously at the weeping Angelica, but was soon hustled out of the room by Julia.

When Julia proffered the smelling salts, Angelica gave her a glance of dislike and waved her away. 'I don't want that disgusting stuff!' she said.

'What is it you do want?' Sir Carey asked.

'You!' she wailed. 'I want you, I always have!'

'Then why did you break our engagement and marry someone else? I still haven't any idea who it is,' he added.

'It isn't anybody! Oh, Carey, don't you understand? It was all a dreadful mistake! Your cousin Daniel told me such awful things about you, and Mama persuaded me that you were not suitable, and he was so very attentive! They kept on at me until I didn't know what I was doing, and eventually I agreed to write to you. But I didn't mean it. Later, when I knew what I'd done, I planned to wait until you came home from Vienna and tell you what a mistake it all was. But you didn't wait! You got married instead! Oh Carey, how could you? It's destroyed my life!'

14

Angelica stayed for a nuncheon of fruit and cold meat. She had calmed down, wiped her eyes, smiled tentatively at Julia and apologized for her outburst.

'I am so ashamed, my lady,' she whispered. 'I love — loved Carey so dearly, and it was such a shock to hear he had forgotten me so soon. I must have been mad at Christmas, but I was missing him so much, and people kept telling me how he was betraying me with other women in Vienna.'

Was that an insinuation that Sir Carey had been making up to her in Vienna, Julia wondered. But she kept her thoughts to herself, and calmly invited Angelica to eat with them before riding back to her home.

'How far away is it?' she asked. 'Won't your parents worry that you are out all day with just a groom?'

'It takes about two hours to ride here, but I am often out all day. I have so many friends, I often call on them and we spend the day together. But I haven't ridden here before, when Carey was at home. I used to come sometimes, before I even met him, to visit

Caroline or Penelope. We were at school together. Did she tell you?'

'Yes. She will be delighted to see you, no doubt.'

Caroline was, to judge by the gush of chatter the two girls indulged in during the meal. Angelica asked numerous questions about mutual schoolfriends, and Caroline, indefatigable correspondent, seemed to know about all their doings. After they had eaten, the two girls wandered outside, and Julia could see their heads bent together as they walked round the rose garden, where the bushes were just beginning to sprout tender new leaves.

Sir Carey came up behind her as she stood in the morning-room window watching.

'I'm so sorry for that exhibition,' he said softly. 'I had no idea she was even at her home, let alone that she would force her way in here.'

'Or that she was not married?' Julia asked, turning to look at him.

'That, too. I wonder what really happened? She was a trifle vague.'

'She's remarkably pretty.' Julia was frowning slightly. Sir Carey had a reminiscent smile on his lips, and her heart sank. He had, after the first shock, appeared pleased to see Angelica. Was he regretting their impulsive marriage? If it had not happened, would Carey and Angelica now be having a grand reconciliation, and planning their wedding?

'I hadn't realized her family home was so close to Courtlands,' she said.

'It is, I suppose, but on the other side of the hills people tend to look westwards for entertainment. They're near enough to Cheltenham to attend assemblies and theatres there. Here we look to Oxford. I never met her in the country, only in London. I've met her parents before, occasionally, but Angelica was at school then.'

He's explaining too much, Julia thought, and her heart sank. He still loves her. She walked to the table and sat down, toying with her pencil as she looked at the lists she had been making. She began to speak, then checked herself. It was too soon. Later they might talk about what could be done.

★　★　★

'Angelica says she had three offers when she was in Yorkshire,' Caroline said the following day. Sir Carey had ridden out early, and Julia was eating breakfast with the two girls.

'Did she say who it was she accepted?' Julia asked. She was aware Sir Carey did not know, and she confessed to herself she was curious to know which man had, if only temporarily, taken Angelica's affections away from him.

'No, she wouldn't tell me. But if I were in London and saw how she behaved towards them all, I could guess,' Caroline said. 'Julia, will you ask Carey if I can have my come out next year? Please!'

'He won't agree,' Julia said, prevaricating.

'He would if you asked him. Julia,' she paused.

'What is it?' Julia asked, resigned, knowing she was unlikely to want to hear more of Caroline's requests.

'I can't dance,' Caroline confessed. 'We learned some country dances at school, and I've danced here in the village at harvest and Christmas, but I don't know any of the dances they do at Almack's. I can't waltz, and they allow it there now. Will you teach me?'

'You can't waltz at Almack's until you are approved by one of the patronesses,' Julia warned. 'But I could teach you to waltz.'

'I'll play the pianoforte for you,' Susan offered. 'But how can you teach Caroline the minuet or cotillion, with just the two of you?'

'Angelica says they have morning dancing classes,' Caroline said eagerly. 'If we could find a few other girls we could do that. Penelope would come.'

'No,' Julia said in haste. 'I'll teach you to

251

waltz, but I cannot teach a whole lot of girls anything more complicated!'

Caroline had to be content, and during the next two weeks, whenever they had time, Julia taught Caroline the steps of the waltz. The girl had a good sense of rhythm, but whatever Julia said could not cure her of excessive swaying of the hips.

'It's fun,' she laughed.

'It makes you look too provincial,' Julia said, but even this did not matter to Caroline.

'Well, I am a provincial, and I won't be otherwise until Carey lets me have my come out!'

★ ★ ★

In London Fanny was in a fever of excitement. When Elizabeth came to ask how she was, Fanny thrust the letter she had been reading towards her.

'Oh, dearest Elizabeth, read that! It's from Frederick, and he's coming home!'

Elizabeth took the letter and read it slowly. 'He's left that wretched Tania, it seems. Will you forgive him?'

Fanny frowned. 'I have no other choice, do I?'

'You need not return to live with him. He could be forced to provide a separate home for you and the children.'

'But if this child,' and she patted her rounded stomach, 'is a boy, he would want to have him brought up at Greystones. He will be Frederick's heir, and it's only right he should be brought up there. Besides, I don't think I would enjoy living on my own.'

Elizabeth nodded. 'I don't think you would, my dear.'

Fanny was twisting the ribbons of her gown round her fingers. 'I keep thinking of Eleonore Metternich. He positively flaunted his affairs in Vienna, and from what I heard there has had mistresses all his life. Yet she endures it, lives with him, shares him with them. At least I'd have the satisfaction of knowing Tania was safely thousands of miles away in Russia. I wouldn't have to share him.'

She watched Elizabeth glance down at the letter and a sudden horrid suspicion assailed her. 'He couldn't be bringing her here, could he?' she demanded. 'He says nothing about her. Oh, Elizabeth, I could forgive him if he came back to me, but it would be so hard if she is anywhere near!'

'We must not assume that. She has big estates in Russia, does she not? There will be matters there which need her attention. I doubt she would wish to come to England. And Frederick says,' she added, waving the letter, 'that he is needed here.'

'He doesn't say he loves me, or is sorry for having betrayed me,' Fanny said, her initial euphoria beginning to wane.

'From what I saw of your husband in Vienna, he was not a demonstrative man, towards you or the children. He may find it difficult to express his feelings.'

Fanny was unconvinced, but she nodded slowly, and took back the letter. 'I shall just have to be patient, and wait until he comes.'

'And take care of yourself for the baby's sake. It does seem as though you can carry it to term now. Sir William says you may get up for an hour or two each day if you are careful. That alone will be a pleasant surprise for him.'

★ ★ ★

Julia rode out with Sir Carey almost every day, and came to know his tenants and their families. They were invited to visit several of the local squires, and dined out with them. Julia asked if she might arrange a dinner party to return the hospitality.

'When do you mean to return to London? Can we fit it in beforehand?'

'We'll go next week. It's a full moon on Wednesday, will that give you sufficient time?'

'I'll send out the invitations at once.'

'Shall we include Caroline? She's growing up, even if I won't agree to her having a Season next year. I was wondering, if you feel it would not be too much for you, if we should take both girls, and Miss Trant, of course, to London with us?'

'She'd be delighted, and I'm sure she'd be on her best behaviour,' Julia said, smiling. 'I enjoy their company, and I am sure Miss Trant will find plenty of educational visits to occupy them.'

'The British Museum, for instance? I'm not sure Caroline would appreciate that! But Susan could go to some concerts. Very well, I'll tell Miss Trant to arrange things.'

The only disturbing thing at Courtlands was Angelica. The girl rode or drove over to see them every two or three days. She sometimes met them when Julia and Sir Carey were out riding and, as this was often in the direction furthest away from her home, Julia was certain the girl deliberately waylaid them. There were no outbursts such as had happened on her first visit, and she seemed to be making an effort to be pleasant to Julia, but Julia was uneasy. The girl was devious, and Sir Carey might begin to regret his hasty marriage. At least he had not suggested inviting Angelica to her dinner party.

On the day of the party Julia stayed in the house to supervise the arrangements. It was an hour before the guests were due to arrive when Caroline came to find her in her dressing-room. Julia had just finished pinning up her hair, in her old style, for Molly was still not a very expert hairdresser, and was trying to decide whether the emeralds Sir Carey had given her were the right jewels to wear with the pale-lilac dress she had chosen. It was a very pretty dress, one she had loved the moment she saw it, with white lace trimming and a cascade of white and lilac ribbons.

Regretfully she laid the emeralds aside. They did not look right, and she would look better with no jewels apart from the belated betrothal ring Sir Carey had given her. She turned to smile at Caroline, who looked quite grown up in a pale-blue gown.

'I like that gown,' she said, but Caroline did not appear to notice.

'Julia, Angelica is here, and her horse is lame. She had to walk the last four miles, which is why she is so late. She can't ride home tonight, and Carey says it's too late to send her back in a carriage.'

'Her parents will be worried!'

'No, they won't, for she was going to stay the night with Penelope at the rectory.'

'Then why can't she go there now?'

'Penelope has one of her migraines, and Angelica says she doesn't want to spend the evening answering questions. You know how the rector is.'

Julia did, and bowed to the inevitable. She nodded, wondering whether this was some devious trick planned by Angelica.

'Shall I ask Foster to lay a place for her at the table? I can lend her an evening gown,' Caroline said.

★ ★ ★

On the day after Angelica's unexpected inclusion in the dinner party Sir Carey said he wanted to travel to London on the following day. 'I need to be there. It's worrying news about Napoleon. Lord Castlereagh writes he would appreciate my advice. We can't be sure some of his former allies might not rejoin Napoleon.'

Julia felt a surge of relief. So he did not wish to remain here, looking forward to the renewed visits Angelica had gaily promised when she finally rode away, on a horse which did not, to Julia, look as though it was at all lame. She had slept badly, considering all night what she ought to do. She admitted she loved Sir Carey, but being with him all the time, when he showed her just normal courtesy, was beginning to be a strain. She had contemplated offering to free him. They could obtain an annulment of the marriage, for it had not been consummated. Then he could marry Angelica. When she dropped into an uneasy doze at dawn she had resolved that was the best way to ensure happiness for both of them. She could resume her former life, once more becoming a companion or governess. He could marry the girl he really loved and wanted.

When Molly brought in her morning chocolate she changed her mind. Angelica was still a child, shallow and interested only in gossip and clothes. She would not make him happy. He would, as any man would, for a time relish the possession of such a lovely girl, but when the initial rapture wore off, could they live happily together? Unless Angelica changed as she grew older, Julia doubted it.

He seemed content with her. He praised her alterations in the house, and she knew she made his life comfortable. That was not enough for her, but it was all she had a right to expect. She would fight for her position as his wife, and perhaps, she thought wistfully, one day he would decide he needed an heir. Then she might become a wife in every sense of the word.

'I can be ready,' she said now. 'I'll begin packing at once.'

★   ★   ★

When they reached London Sir Carey went straight to the Foreign Office to see Lord Castlereagh, while Julia supervised the unpacking and then went to read the correspondence and invitations which had been delivered that morning. She recognized Fanny's handwriting, and saw that it was unusually uneven. Breaking the wafer she began to read.

The note was short, telling her only that Frederick was coming home, and begging Julia to visit her as soon as she was back in London.

Sir Carey had told her to accept those invitations she wanted, so she wrote hurried notes of acceptance to hostesses begging their presence at balls and receptions. The Season was in full swing, and there were parties every night. She would need to buy more gowns. But first she would go and see how Fanny did.

Elizabeth met her in the hall and beckoned her into the empty dining-room.

'She is pinning her hopes on a full reconciliation,' she told Julia. 'I've tried to convince her he must have finished with that wretched Russian Countess, and I think she believes it now. Having read his letter, though, I've been wondering. He doesn't say so. Nor does he show any hint of remorse, or say a word of apology. I hope you'll try to keep her hopes and spirits up.'

'Of course I will. Frederick is not the man ever to admit to having made a mistake, or to offer an apology, particularly to a woman, so I don't see anything strange in that.'

'You know him better than I do. I'm relieved, I admit. I have been worried, and in some ways I hope he does not arrive too soon. The longer she has without any disappointment, the more chance she has of keeping this child.'

'We'll all encourage her. Elizabeth, I have a favour to ask. I need more clothes. Will you help me choose some?'

'You need to have some made. I'll send my own dressmaker to you, but I will happily help you to select materials and all the other things you must buy, like fans and shawls and slippers. Shall we do that tomorrow? Another thing. Will you want vouchers for Almack's?'

'Sir Carey hasn't said. Will he want to go there? Isn't it mainly for debutantes and prospective husbands to meet? That's what it was when I had my own Season. Not that it found me a husband,' she added, recalling the many young men who had paid attentions to her, and rapidly retreated when they discovered she had no fortune, not even a modest dowry.

'The Marriage Mart? Yes, it still is, and most other people find it amazingly dull. But some of the patronesses were in Vienna, you may enjoy meeting them again. Now you had better go up to Fanny. Come and have a nuncheon with me afterwards.'

As Julia bent to kiss Fanny, who was reclining on a day bed, she thought her sister looked unhealthily flushed. Her eyes glittered, and she felt too hot for comfort.

'Dear Julia, I'm so glad to see you. I am so bored having to rest all the time, and with so few people bothering to visit me. They come once, but when they hear about Frederick they avoid me. But when he is back it will be different.'

'I think you imagine that, dear. It's the Season, there is so much going on, people don't have the time. Do you recall when I came out, and we were going to three or four parties every night, as well as all the rides and drives and morning visits?'

Fanny sighed. 'I wish I knew when he would be coming. He didn't say, in the letter, where he was, so I cannot even make a guess at the time he will take to travel back to England. Here, read it,' she added, pulling a crumpled sheet of paper from under the cushion she'd been lying against.

Julia took the letter, and though she was used to Frederick's terse manner of correspondence, she decided that Elizabeth was right to be concerned. There were no words of affection for Fanny or the girls, and very little information beyond the bare fact he was coming to England. He did not even refer to it as home.

Fanny was still thinking of the parties she was missing. 'I wish I could go out and meet people,' she repeated. 'I want to discover what is happening, with such excitement about Napoleon's escape, people wondering whether the wars will start all over again.'

'Don't you read the newspapers?'

'Yes, but that's not the same as talking to people who really know, as we could in Vienna.'

'I'll bring you any news I hear. And you will be fit again before Christmas. There will be next year's Season to look forward to. You have to think of the baby now. Is everything all right?'

'They say so, and this time I am hopeful. When I lost the others it was always earlier than this. But tell me your news. How is Sir

Carey? What is Courtlands like? Do you get on with his sisters?'

Julia did her best to describe Sir Carey's home, being careful not to mention the attacks on her, or the visit of the unmarried Angelica. They had not moved in the same circles before, so she hoped none of Fanny's visitors knew about the girl and her activities.

'You look tired,' she said after a while. 'I'll go now, but I'll come back whenever I can, and if I hear any interesting news I'll be sure to tell you.'

★ ★ ★

'Wellington is in Brussels now, so we shall see some action,' Sir Carey told Julia that evening. They were dining quietly at home, and he was complimentary about the dinner she had ordered. 'The armies are preparing, and are expected to meet soon.'

He was debating with himself whether he ought to go to Brussels, or even rejoin the army which he had left seven years ago after his father died, before the war in the Peninsula had begun. Wellington needed all the support he could find, since the actions of the other powers might be in doubt. It was, too, a ragbag army, with many foreigners, since many of the best troops were still in the

Americas. Castlereagh had advised him to wait, saying there might be tasks he could perform more usefully in England. Sir Carey hoped these did not involve travel to consult the other powers.

'Will the Congress end now?' Julia asked.

'Apparently not. Most of the negotiations are finished, just a few smaller matters to be settled. How was your sister? And what entertainments are we promised?'

'I have put the invitations in your study. As for Fanny, she was a little feverish, I thought, but that might be accounted for by the news of Frederick's return.'

'So the man has admitted he was wrong?'

'Not in so many words.' Julia explained about the doubts she'd had when reading Frederick's letter. 'It has cheered Fanny, though, and if she is happy the child is less at risk, I'm sure.'

'It seems strange, but I have not yet seen her since we married. Is she well enough for me to call?'

'She would welcome more visitors.'

'Then I suppose I ought to ask formally for your hand,' he said, grinning.

'She's not my guardian!' Julia protested. 'I'm of age, and she never was my guardian.'

'I'll make it a courtesy call.'

'She said she was anxious for more news,

so I'm sure she would welcome whatever you can tell her. I suppose, if Frederick is travelling back from somewhere in Russia, he won't become involved with the fighting?'

'He is probably only a few days after his letter. And we don't know where he went. No, if he's in Prussia or the Netherlands now he'll be perfectly safe. People are remaining in Brussels, even. Many of the English went there once Napoleon had abdicated, and seem to be having a good time, so they don't wish to leave.'

I hope their faith in Wellington is justified, he thought to himself. 'The Duke is a very successful commander, but so is Napoleon. They have not yet met face to face. The Allies must be persuaded to send troops.'

'Surely they will. They won't want to return to what it was like before, endless fighting.'

'We must hope so. I'll go and see Lady Cunningham tomorrow,' he said. 'An excellent dinner, my dear, but I fear I must leave you now as I have people to see.'

★   ★   ★

Julia spent the following morning shopping with Elizabeth. They visited warehouses for fabrics, and Julia tried not to be swept away with the choice. In Bond Street they found slippers and shawls and fans and reticules which would match the gowns. The carriage was full of parcels by the time they returned to Upper Brook Street.

'Now you must rest this afternoon,' Elizabeth said. 'You are going to the Hawkins's reception tonight. It's your first public appearance with Sir Carey, and you must look your best.'

Julia nodded. She was apprehensive. 'They'll all want to see what sort of woman he married.'

'Of course. Now what are you going to wear? The pale-green gown you bought when you were first in London would be ideal, and the new dark-green slippers.'

Julia agreed to all Elizabeth's suggestions, even permitting her to send round her own maid to do Julia's hair.

'Molly is a reliable maid, but she does not have the skills you need yet, if you are to look as beautiful as you can be.'

'Me? Beautiful?' Julia asked. 'I'm just passable.'

She was not nearly as pretty as Angelica, she thought with a pang. She could not compete with the girl on looks or vivacity. The notion of competition had not previously occurred to her, but as she rested on her bed that afternoon, in obedience to Elizabeth's orders, she began to wonder if it would be possible. What assets did she have that she might employ to tempt her husband away from his former love? She began ticking them off on her fingers. Perhaps most importantly she had the great advantage of living in the same house. She was older, and, she hoped, wiser. She could keep house, and already Sir Carey was admiring her changes. He was gentleman enough to support her in public, she was sure. The only times Angelica could be sure of meeting him would be at public assemblies, and in other houses, but Julia hoped these occasions would be few. He had said their two families looked in opposite directions for local amusements, and since he had not met her as an adult before she came to London, it was unlikely they would have mutual friends in the neighbourhood who would invite them to the same local parties. She might ride over to Courtlands when they were there, but Sir Carey was often out during the day, on estate business. Would Angelica try to waylay him? Probably; she seemed a shameless girl. Surely he would see through such wiles and if he was the sort of honourable man she thought, he would come to dislike such blatant attention.

By the time it was necessary to dress for the evening Julia was feeling confident she could manage affairs so that Sir Carey began to appreciate the advantages of being married to her, rather than to a lovely but shallow and much younger girl. When Sir Carey complimented her on her looks and insisted she wear a diamond necklace which had belonged to his mother, she was looking forward to the evening, ready to face Society at his side.

Her confidence waned slightly when they entered the large room where the reception was taking place. It seemed to be crowded with fashionable people, and though she looked round eagerly she could see none of the acquaintances she had known in Vienna.

They all stared so! She'd been ignored most of the time at the Viennese balls, just a poor relation of Lady Cunningham, who herself was of little importance compared with all the European royalty and nobility attending. Later, of course, there had been the calumnies of Mrs Webber, which had caused some people to look askance at her, but she had done her best to ignore them. Perhaps it was the story of their marriage, curiosity about it, which so intrigued people. Julia threw her head up high and smiled brilliantly. Then the smile froze on her lips. Stepping from behind a group of older women was Angelica, and she was walking towards them, her hands held out, and a charming smile on her face.

15

'So you are back.'

Fanny turned her head away as Frederick bent to kiss her, and the kiss landed on her cheek. She was determined not to make this easy for him. She did not know herself, even, what she wanted. Elizabeth had advised her to be cool and judge by Frederick's words and actions whether he had truly repented, whether she felt she could ever bear to live with him again. Fanny was determined to follow that advice, for she knew that if she did not, and gave way at once, she would always be treated as negligible.

'You don't seem very pleased to see me,' he said petulantly.

'Why should I be? You deserted us in Vienna and went off with that trollop, heaven knows where, and never bothered to inform me where you were or even whether you would be returning home.'

'The posts are difficult. And why are you here, imposing on Mr and Mrs Pryce, instead of being at Greystones, looking after things there?'

'You have a perfectly capable steward, and

I am here in an attempt to carry this child to term, for you!' Fanny snapped, patting her stomach. Her condition had been hidden until now by the loose, flowing robe she had carefully draped across her lap. 'Do you want an heir? Or are you proposing to return to Russia and spend the rest of your life there?'

Frederick looked startled. 'You're breeding?' he asked. 'In that case, you must come home. It is mine, I suppose?'

Fanny stared at him in disgust. Never before, despite his own infidelities, had he questioned her behaviour. 'Please go! If you cannot be civil to me, I want no more to do with you!'

He looked momentarily abashed. 'Well,' he said, 'I could hardly blame you, could I? A good many children are fathered by men other than the husbands. It's the norm in the *ton* from all we hear. Look at Lady Melbourne. A different father for every child, from what they say.'

'I don't wish to look at anyone but myself! Are you going back to Russia?'

He shuddered. 'It's a barbarous country, even in the area close to the west. Lord knows what it's like further eastwards.'

Fanny frowned. 'So that's why you came home? Because you were uncomfortable? That's not very flattering. I'm prepared to accept you no longer want me, but surely your daughters mean something to you? And if this child is a boy, you'll have your heir at last.'

'When have I said I no longer want you?' he replied, attempting to take her hand. Fanny resolutely moved it away.

'Your actions say it.'

Frederick rubbed a hand over his eyes. 'Fanny, I'm exhausted with travelling. I don't want arguments. I want you and the girls to come home.'

'That is impossible. I'm forbidden to move about or do much, for fear of losing the baby. And I don't want to come home with you. I want a formal separation.'

★ ★ ★

Julia took a deep breath and smiled brilliantly. 'Why, Angelica, how lovely to see you again so soon,' she said, in a clear, carrying voice. 'You didn't say you were coming to London the other day at Courtlands.'

'I didn't know,' Angelica said. 'Papa only told me when I got home from seeing you.'

'The day after you stayed with us?'

She heard Sir Carey, standing slightly behind her, utter a slight choking sound, and smiled.

'Where are your parents?' Sir Carey broke in. 'We must pay our respects to them, and I want to introduce Julia to all my friends.'

Angelica, her smile rather fixed, told them her parents were in one of the other salons, and with a smile and a nod Sir Carey took Julia's arm and steered her in that direction, leaving Angelica looking after them.

'Best get it over with,' he murmured in Julia's ear. 'I wonder if they were hoping Angelica and I could take up from where we left off?'

Was he regretting they could not? His manners were so impeccable Julia could not tell. Perhaps meeting Angelica's parents would give her some clue.

Julia saw at once where Angelica's beauty came from. Mrs Philpot was in her mid thirties, but looked younger. She was also blonde and blue-eyed, slender enough for the fashionably slim skirt to cling provocatively to her excellent figure. The neckline was daringly low, and her breasts had been pushed up, Julia was convinced, by her stays, though these were so cleverly designed no evidence of them was visible through the silk of her gown.

Mr Philpot, beside her, was in his late fifties, corpulent and red-faced. He glared at Sir Carey and merely nodded to Julia when she was introduced. Mrs Philpot began to smile, and then shook her head.

'Dear Sir Carey, who would ever have thought that a confirmed bachelor such as yourself would feel Cupid's dart twice in such a short time? Angelica was devastated when she heard of your marriage.'

'Perhaps Angelica should have had more faith in me,' he replied evenly.

'Oh, but she is so young! And she felt deserted. You must admit it was hard on a girl only just out of the schoolroom to find what she imagined was true devotion, and then discover that the pleasures of Vienna meant more to you than she did.'

'She found consolation, I heard.'

'That was just a passing phase, caused by her loneliness.' She turned to Julia, who had been standing by, ignored while this barbed exchange took place, and looked her up and down. 'When I heard Sir Carey had married so suddenly, I expected him to have chosen a girl who looked like my own dear child.'

'I think he wanted a change, not to be constantly reminded of his disappointment in her,' Julia said sweetly. 'Do tell me, who was it who turned her affections away from Sir Carey? He must have had some very enticing attractions.'

'Oh, that's all over now. A momentary

attraction when she was vulnerable. But she will make an excellent marriage, you may be sure. Already there are some exceedingly eligible men looking interested, and we have been in London but a couple of days.'

'I wish her good fortune,' Julia said, 'like mine.'

★ ★ ★

Fanny cried herself to sleep that night, after Frederick's visit. Had she driven him away? Did she want that? When Elizabeth had advised her to be cool and distant, she had thought it good advice. Now she was not so sure. Frederick was a proud man. He'd looked astounded when she'd asked for a separation. Instead of blustering, trying to persuade her to change her mind, he'd stared at her, then without a further word turned and left the room.

She'd been tempted to run after him and tell him she didn't mean it, but before she could reach the door it opened again and Elizabeth came in.

'He looked shattered, my dear. Did you ask for a separation?'

'Yes, but it's probably what he wants! Oh, Elizabeth, I shouldn't have done that!'

'Nonsense, of course you should. The man

deserves a shock to bring him to his senses. Wait and see what he does now.'

'He'll probably divorce me.'

She was still in bed after breakfast the next day when Elizabeth brought her a huge bouquet of flowers.

'From your husband. You see, he's taken heed. He sent me a note asking if he could call this afternoon. He's prepared to be conciliatory. So we must get rid of those red eyes and you must remain firm. Don't fall on his neck and beg pardon.'

Fanny almost smiled. It was probably what she would have done had Elizabeth not been here to stiffen her resolve. She nodded submissively. Elizabeth, though perfectly happily married to her Edward, seemed to know all about the feminine tricks Fanny had never acquired. She would abide by her advice.

'Do I insist on a separation still? He might think I mean it and agree.'

'Hint that you would be willing to negotiate.'

Fanny chuckled. 'Like the Powers in Vienna?' she said. 'Do you think I should call on someone like Lord Castlereagh to present my case?'

'You are fully capable of doing that yourself,' Elizabeth reassured her. 'Mention the children, how they have almost forgotten their father, and need to see him frequently so that they know him. Say a son and heir should be brought up in the home he will one day inherit, but how sad it would be for a baby to be separated from its mother. Especially, you may hint, if its father means to leave it there without him too. And you might say, should he wish to divorce you, that step-mothers are notoriously unkind to the children of a first wife, and if they have children of their own, jealous of the first brood.'

Fanny smiled. 'I think I might even enjoy this,' she said. 'You are so kind to me, such a good friend, and I have imposed on your generosity for far too long.'

'And you must stay here until you have reached a satisfactory conclusion.'

★ ★ ★

Though she contrived not to show it, Julia's peace was seriously disturbed during the next few weeks. Everywhere they went she seemed to meet Angelica. Whether it was a ball or reception, a concert or balloon ascent, Angelica was nearby. She did not always speak to them, but Julia could sense her watchfulness. When Caroline and Susan accompanied them, Angelica would come and talk to Caroline, and the two girls were frequently to be found with their heads close together, gossiping and laughing.

Sir Carey seemed to treat her with indulgence. Frequently, when Julia saw him watching Angelica, she surprised a small twisted smile on his lips. The girl still enchanted him, it was clear, and although he gave her no hint of his true feelings, no doubt he regretted his hasty marriage.

A different irritant was Mrs Webber. Several instances of her malicious remarks were repeated to Julia. Surely this could not all be ascribed to her friendship with Frau Gunter, and that old woman's threat that Julia would regret tangling with her? Julia tried to recall all the occasions when they had met in Vienna. She had avoided the woman whenever possible, and so had Fanny. Was that the reason for this sustained malevolence?

Mr Webber was, she now knew, Austrian by birth. Did Frau Gunter have some sort of hold on him? It seemed possible.

Then Julia recalled the meeting at the inn in Bavaria, when Sir Carey had told her she was being offensive, and refused to allow them to share his private parlour. Surely if that was what had caused this attitude, she ought to be spreading rumours about Sir Carey?

One evening, after Julia had been snubbed by a particular crony of Mrs Webber's, which Sir Carey had witnessed, he tackled Julia when they reached home.

'Come into the library. Foster, you need not stay up. Now, my dear, what is the reason for that harpy's hostility towards you? Is she the only one? Does it happen often?'

Julia shook her head. 'I believe it's the doing of Mrs Webber, but I cannot understand why she is so persistent. Frau Gunter may have instigated the gossip in Vienna, to punish me for arguing with her. She said I would regret it. But that fails to explain why Mrs Webber is so vindictive towards me still. From what I have heard, and from what a few people we knew in Vienna have told me, she is spreading rumours that I trapped you into marriage.'

'It must be more than that,' Sir Carey said.

Julia hesitated. 'She may have resented not being permitted to share the parlour, where — where you told her we were betrothed,' she said slowly. She hadn't wanted to appear to blame him, but they had to consider all possibilities.

'That's a poor reason. There must be something else. Leave it to me, Julia. I have an idea, and need to make some enquiries. But I will stop her tongue one way or another.'

'Maybe the only way is to cut it out! Thank you. I confess she makes me uncomfortable, when I should be revelling in the Season, and enjoying all the new clothes and other gifts you are lavishing on me.'

'You deserve them, for you are making my life more comfortable than it has been for years. Look at the new curtains you have had made in this house. It looks better than ever before. I will deal with Mrs Webber.'

*   *   *

It took Sir Carey two days and numerous enquiries of friends, and a visit to an insalubrious office in the City before he acquired the information he needed. When he did, he gave a satisfied nod and set off for the house the Webbers had hired in Mount Street.

'Is Mr Webber at home?' he asked the footman who answered his knock on the door.

'He's at White's, I believe,' the footman replied.

'Thank you.'

Sir Carey was thoughtful as he walked

towards St James's Street. It was fortunate he would be able to confront Mr Webber on neutral territory. He hadn't relished the possibility of a shrill Mrs Webber joining in what would be a difficult encounter.

He found Mr Webber ensconced in one of the deep armchairs in the club reading a copy of *The Times*. Fortunately no one else was in earshot, so Sir Carey dropped into a chair facing, and called for a bottle of claret.

'Join me, sir?' he asked.

Mr Webber nodded cautiously and lowered the newspaper. 'Thank you, Evelegh.'

When they both had full glasses Sir Carey leant forward. 'Mr Webber, this is a delicate matter. It has come to my attention that your wife is making slanderous allegations about mine. I ask you to control her, and do what you can to refute these slanders. Or Mrs Webber will regret it, and lose what credit she has with the *ton*. I know she craves acceptance, but I have high connections. I can make life exceedingly difficult for her.'

'I don't know what you mean! My wife isn't slandering anyone!'

'You are blustering, sir. You know full well the malicious gossip she is spreading, and I believe I know the reason. Her brother John was at a house party near York at Christmas, was he not? He is an intimate of my own cousin, Daniel Fitzhugh, who was also there, and who has his own reasons for preventing my marriage. Between them they induced Angelica Philpot to break off her engagement to me, and accept a proposal from John. He's a plausible rogue, but he has no income apart from a hundred pounds a year, and I hear he loses much of that in gambling debts. He's being pursued by the moneylenders. To him Angelica's portion would seem a fortune, and she was ripe for the picking. I thought at first she had been tempted by a title greater than mine, but now I know better. Then she changed her mind, and he wanted revenge, but if he targeted her it would be obvious why, even though they have kept the news of that brief engagement quiet. So he blames me, and my wife. It is hardly logical, but then his debts are such I doubt he sleeps much at night, and his wits have gone begging. He and his sister, who began a campaign of slander while she was in Vienna, for a different reason at first, are trying to hurt Julia. I will not have it, sir. If you cannot control your wife, be assured I will bring a suit for slander against her. That will hardly improve her standing.'

Mr Webber had reddened during this speech, and for a full minute he did not reply.

'You must know how difficult it is to control a woman's tongue,' he said at last. 'I assure you, I have no hand in it, and it embarrasses me. But what can I do?'

'Take her home. Tell her that if she will not go she will soon be in court. And her precious brother might find himself there too. Or in the Fleet. I could buy some of his debts, and have no illusions, sir, I would use them.'

★ ★ ★

Julia was visiting Fanny when Elizabeth came up to say Frederick was asking to see his wife.

'Don't go, Julia,' Fanny said in panic. She did not relish the prospect of seeing Frederick alone.

'You cannot talk to him properly with me here,' Julia said gently. 'Fanny, be firm. He's showing contrition by sending you all these flowers.'

Fanny looked round the room and giggled. 'It does look rather like a florist's shop, doesn't it?'

Elizabeth laughed. 'Your husband seems unusually anxious to see you, Fanny. We've denied him for a few days, but I think it's time you listened to what he has to say.'

Fanny sighed. 'I suppose I must. But I'm afraid I'll give in if he's as conciliatory and apologetic as his letters have been.'

'Say you'll consider and reply in a few

days,' Julia advised. 'I'll go. I have to purchase a mask for the masquerade we attend tonight.'

Elizabeth left too, and a few minutes later Frederick entered the room.

'You look pretty today,' he said, and Fanny felt herself blush with pleasure. It had been a long time since Frederick had paid her compliments. 'They said you'd been ill. Not the child, I trust?'

'Do you care only for the child?' Fanny asked, her initial pleasure at seeing him in this mood diminished.

'Of course not. Fanny, let us stop this fencing. I know you'll come back to me in the end, so why not admit it?'

'I am not so sure, Frederick. I need some guarantees, that you will treat me always with consideration. You made me look very stupid in Vienna, while you were chasing that trollop.'

'I know, and I'm sorry. I was bewitched, but I promise it will not happen again. I'd grown used to you, Fanny, I took you for granted. It will not happen again, I swear. I want you and the children back at home with me.'

Fanny looked hard at him, and saw he meant it. She was tempted to throw herself into his arms and tell him there was nothing she wanted more, but the words of Julia and Elizabeth stopped her.

'I will consider,' she said. 'But I cannot yet travel, Sir William insists I do no more than walk about these rooms until the child is born.'

'If I hired a house nearby, could you be moved there? We can stay in London as long as necessary. When will the child be born?'

'Not until October. I don't want to stay in London during the summer, but Elizabeth says they will remain until Napoleon is dealt with, and I would be welcome to stay here afterwards, should they go to the country before October.'

'You would be better in your own house, with your own servants. Mr Pryce told me his coachman and your maid will be here in a few days. They sent a message from Brussels.'

'Maggie? Here? That's good news,' Fanny said.

'So you could be perfectly comfortable in our own house. The girl will do anything for you.'

'I'll consider it,' Fanny repeated. 'But London is crowded, Julia tells me. People are waiting for news of Napoleon. There may not be houses available.'

'If you'll forgive me, I'll find one somehow.'

Some days before, Julia had confessed she had never attended a masquerade during her one London Season. 'It was not considered proper,' she said, laughing.

'Then we will go to one.'

Sir Carey had hired a box, and for a while Julia was content to sit and watch the masked dancers in their dominoes. She thought she recognized a few people, but it was difficult to be sure. Then they danced, and Julia basked in his full attention. Here there was no need for Sir Carey to observe the conventions and ask other girls to dance. He had ordered a supper in their box, and Julia was sipping at champagne when something about one of the dancers made her look closely.

'Carey,' she exclaimed, unaware that for the first time she had omitted his title. 'Look at the girl in the pale-pink domino. I'm convinced it's Caroline!'

'Caroline? How can you be sure?'

'When I taught her to waltz, she would sway about like that. Very few women do. They move their upper bodies, but they don't usually swing their — their lower bodies . . . about with quite so much abandon!' Julia said, blushing.

At that moment a young man, somewhat

the worse for drink, touched the girl they were watching on the shoulder. Laughing, her partner gave her up, and she moved away, held more tightly than was seemly in the other man's arms.

'Stay here, I will deal with this,' Sir Carey said, his voice grim.

He vaulted over the low wall which bordered the box, and marched across the dance floor to intercept the pair, who were now almost galloping round the room rather than performing the waltz.

The man objected vociferously to Sir Carey's attempts to halt them, until the girl broke away from him and ran across the ballroom. She was heading in Julia's direction, and Julia moved swiftly to intercept her.

She grasped the girl's arm, and Caroline, for it was she, gasped in fright.

'Come with me,' Julia said, and almost dragged Caroline back to their box. By this time Sir Carey, having dismissed the erstwhile partner with a few choice words, had joined them. 'Sit down, calm yourself, and then tell us what you are doing here,' she said calmly.

Caroline gulped, and made to remove her mask in order to wipe the tears from her eyes. Julia held out a hand to stop her. 'Don't be foolish. You don't want to risk being recognized.'

'Who brought you here?' Sir Carey asked, and Julia could feel the suppressed fury in his voice.

Caroline shook her head. 'I won't tell you!'

'Very well, you will go straight back to Courtlands.'

'Oh no! Please, Carey, I won't do it again,' Caroline pleaded.

'Who was it? Some infatuated youth? Though how you've met any I can't imagine.'

'It was Angelica, and two of the men she knows,' Caroline whispered. 'She said it would show me a little of what entertainments there are in London. I didn't think it was wrong!'

'Not wrong? To sneak out of the house without telling me or Julia where you were going with two men you don't know! Have you no sense of propriety? Has Miss Trant not taught you better? I think, my girl, you need to be sent to a really severe school where you might learn a little decorum, and try to behave as a well-brought up young lady.'

Caroline grasped his hand. 'Don't blame Miss Trant,' she said, beginning to sob in earnest. 'Indeed, Carey, I know it was wrong, but when Angelica suggested it I couldn't resist. I promise I won't do it again, if you let me stay in London.'

'You will go to Courtlands as soon as I can arrange it. Now we will go home.'

'I must tell Angelica where I am,' Caroline protested. 'She'll be frantic with worry if I don't!'

'That young woman can look after herself, I am learning. Come, and try to hold your head up. We don't want everyone staring at you.'

16

Sir Carey had spent all day at the Foreign Office. The previous night he had meant to make arrangements to send Caroline and Susan home with Miss Trant today, but Lord Castlereagh had sent for him early in the morning.

Caroline had sulked all the way home from the masquerade the previous evening. She had rushed up to her room without a word, and he had shrugged and let her go. Julia had touched his arm and said not to worry, girls took things hard, and she would no doubt be more herself in the morning. He had not discovered whether she was right, for Caroline had not been up when he left the house. She was probably in bed now, since it was late, and she would no doubt be anxious to avoid him. He did not much care. The news from Brussels was bad. Napoleon's army was growing larger by the day. Many of the old regiments had changed sides and joined him, and he was moving northwards. He had no time to spare for rebellious sisters. Thank heaven for Julia, who would know how to deal with her.

Julia had retired, Foster told him when he arrived home. Sir Carey nodded and climbed the stairs to his own room. He wondered for a moment whether to go to Julia, but he had never been into her bedroom here, though at this house their rooms were separated only by his own dressing-room. Then he shook his head. He had promised her he would make no demands. They could talk in the morning, and he would send Caroline home straight away.

Tanner was waiting for him in his dressing room, and Sir Carey undressed swiftly. He dismissed the man and put on his night robe. He spent a few minutes writing a letter to his steward at Courtlands, and then picked up the candle and walked through to his bedroom.

Setting the candle down on the night table he pulled aside the curtains, and blinked. There was someone in his bed. For a moment his heart leapt as he wondered if Julia, for some reason of her own, had invaded his privacy, and then he saw that the curls peeping from beneath the covers were paler than Julia's bright locks. He snatched up the candle and bent closer.

'Just what the devil do you think you are doing?' he demanded.

Angelica smiled lazily up at him. 'I came to

you, my love. I thought it was time to stop this silly game.'

'Get out! You'll go home at once, and I never want to see you again. By heavens, I had a fortunate escape when you jilted me!'

She stared up at him, disbelief and anger striving for supremacy in her face. 'But you love me!' she almost screamed. 'Carey, it was all a mistake! Mrs Webber told me you know it was her brother. He and your cousin kept telling me of the women you had in Vienna. They made me think you were unfaithful, and I only meant to show you I didn't care, to make you come and plead with me to forgive you! I never meant to marry him!'

She had struggled out of the bed and ran towards him. She was naked, and had drenched herself with the strong perfume she favoured. He grasped her arms and shook her. 'You she-devil! Who helped you? How did you get in here without anyone seeing you?'

'I won't tell you! Carey, you can get an annulment, and then we could be wed as we planned. Please! Carey, I love you so much!'

She fell as he released her and moved away, then she began to crawl towards him, moaning his name continuously.

He turned and saw Julia standing in the doorway.

'I heard the commotion,' she said quietly. 'I'll find her a wrap.'

Angelica saw her and began to hurl abuse at her.

'You're not a real wife,' she shouted. 'You've never shared a bed! It's not a proper marriage. Tanner told my father's valet, and he told Papa, and I heard him and Mama talking about it, saying you should get an annulment, because that woman trapped you, but it's not a real marriage. You could still marry me!'

'You are the last girl I would ever marry,' he said, 'and unless you agree to leave now, I'll carry you back to your home just as you are.'

Julia returned bringing one of her own dressing robes, and a small phial. Between them they wrapped the robe round Angelica, and Julia pushed her to sit on the bed.

'Take this, it will calm you,' she ordered, and poured something into a small glass. Meekly Angelica obeyed.

'Where are your clothes?' Julia asked, and Angelica gestured towards the far side of the bed.

'Behind the curtains. I hid them. I hid under the bed when the maid came to turn it down.'

She seemed to have collapsed, all her

furious energy gone. She permitted Julia to dress her, while Julia asked questions.

'Who helped you? Was it Caroline?'

She nodded. 'I persuaded her to. She said she wanted to pay you back for recognizing her at the masquerade.'

Julia turned to Sir Carey. 'Can you go and find a hackney? Best not use your own carriage. We can take her home, and perhaps no one need know.' She turned to Angelica, who was now weeping quietly. 'If we cannot return you to your parents your reputation will be completely ruined, so you had best co-operate.'

★ ★ ★

It was some time before Sir Carey, Julia and Angelica were dressed and able to slip down the back stairs into the garden. Julia waited with the girl while Sir Carey went to fetch a hackney, which they clambered into at the end of the road. She was wondering exactly what Sir Carey would do to Caroline for this latest escapade.

Angelica seemed to revive slightly as they drove towards her house.

'Let me out at the end of the road. I can get into the house without anyone knowing.'

'Think again,' Sir Carey told her. 'I am

coming in to inform your parents of what you have been doing. Then it is their business, but I hope they take you back to the country and don't permit you to set foot in London for several years, until you have grown up and can be trusted to behave responsibly.'

'I only wanted to live in a castle,' she said, bursting into tears. 'It wasn't you I wanted, but your house. It was so romantic, to have a real castle for a home.'

'Then I suggest you try to find a man who has a real one he actually lives in,' Julia said. 'Sir Carey's is little more than a picturesque ruin, but there are inhabited ones.'

'Especially in Scotland,' Sir Carey added. 'That might be far enough away.'

Roused from their beds, Angelica's parents greeted them with astonishment and dismay. Sir Carey told them exactly what had occurred, and when Mrs Philpot began to say Angelica was a good girl and would never have behaved in such a fashion, he was exaggerating and being vindictive because she had jilted him, Julia quietly told her she had witnessed all of it.

'What's more, she has been trying to insinuate herself into our home,' she added. 'She meets us when we are out riding, she comes to Courtlands on the flimsiest excuse, and I am getting tired of it. She is a nuisance, and it is time she was taught a little decorum. I hope you will see to it.'

They left soon afterwards, and as it was only a short distance to Upper Brook Street Sir Carey suggested they walked.

'I think we will be safe enough,' he said. 'The moon's full, and though London has a reputation for ruffians, there are still plenty of people about.'

At that moment a clock began to chime the hours and they stood and counted.

'Eleven,' Sir Carey said. 'Thank you, Julia, for your help.' He tucked her hand through his arm and they began to stroll companionably homewards.

Julia was thinking of the harsh words he had uttered towards Angelica. If he meant them, and they had not been fury at the situation she had created, it appeared he had got over his infatuation for the girl. She might have felt sorry for Angelica but for the girl's claim that it was the castle she wanted, not Sir Carey. Had she meant it?

Sir Carey must have been thinking similar thoughts. 'Romantic little fool,' he said. 'But Caroline goes home tomorrow.'

'Do you want me to go with her?' Julia asked.

'Of course not. I need you here. Miss Trant can deal with her. If I know Caroline she will by now be quaking with fear, aghast at what she did.'

Julia gave a sigh of relief. She'd had to offer, but she had no desire to be closeted with a resentful Caroline who would probably try to blame her for her ills.

★ ★ ★

Frederick appeared at the Pryces' house looking triumphant. 'I have a house, and it's only just round the corner,' he told Fanny. 'So will you agree to move into it?'

'I thought it was impossible to hire one this year,' Fanny said.

'Yes, but the Webbers, who had hired this house for the Season, suddenly have to go home. I didn't understand why, but they were anxious to be gone, and only too pleased to sell me the rest of the lease. I can renew it next month until Christmas, the agent tells me, so if we have to stay here until the child is born, we have our own home until then.'

'And the rest? The other women?' Fanny asked, trying not to show her feelings too plainly.

'The rest? Oh, Fanny, I was a fool, and I admit it, and I promise there will be no more such incidents to vex you. So will you forgive me and come back to me?'

'If Sir William says I can move, yes, I will,' Fanny said, and smiled secretly as Frederick kissed her. Would this husband whom she loved despite his faults now treat her more carefully?

When Julia called later in the day to see how she was Fanny could barely contain her excitement.

'He truly has repented,' she insisted.

'I hope so,' Julia said, kissing her sister. 'But you need to remember not to give way to him all the time, or he could forget and begin to treat you with little consideration, as he did before.'

'He won't,' Fanny said confidently. 'I know how to deal with him now. I hope Sir William will let me move. How fortunate the Webbers had to go home, and their house is only just round the corner. Elizabeth says the girls can continue to have lessons here with Miss Jenkins, so I don't have the trouble of finding a governess for them. It's all happening for the best. And if I have a son Frederick will be so pleased he'll do anything for me!'

★ ★ ★

Sir Carey was thoughtful as he walked back to Upper Brook Street from the Foreign Office. He had been into the city to consult with his man of business, for he needed to make a will and provide Julia with a regular dress allowance and pin money, instead of handing her rolls of bills whenever she needed money. She had by now been able to set up accounts with various milliners and mantua makers, but a more regular arrangement was called for. When he left the office he noticed considerable excitement around the Exchange. The stock jobbers were scurrying about, full of suppressed excitement, and he heard an occasional word. 'Victory' and 'Wellington' were amongst them, and he began to hope that this was good news of the long-awaited battle. He had called a hackney and driven to Whitehall, but no one at the Foreign Office had any official news. Perhaps they would hear more later in the day.

He and Julia were invited to a ball that evening at the house of one of his old friends, another former Guards officer who had been wounded at Badajoz. She was wearing a new gown, of creamy satin embroidered on the bodice and along the hem with green and gold flowers. She had green slippers, and wore the emerald necklace, ear-rings and bracelets he had given her. Her honey-coloured hair was drawn back into a neat chignon, with ringlets escaping to fall either side of her face and on to her shoulders.

She had a serene beauty, he thought as he handed her into their carriage. Her delicate bone structure would ensure that it lasted, whereas the youthful prettiness of Angelica would probably fade in a few years. He shook his head. He was finished with Angelica. Her actions had given him a disgust of her. Throughout Julia had been calm and dignified, ready with help and suggestions for dealing with problems. His marriage had been hasty and unconsidered, but it was one of the best things he had done. It remained to convince Julia of that, and he cursed inwardly that he had promised her not to demand marital rights. He frequently found he wanted, most desperately, to take her to bed and make love to her all night.

'You are preoccupied,' she commented as they drove along Piccadilly.

Hastily he dragged his thoughts away from the pleasures of being in bed with Julia.

'I think there is news from Brussels,' he said. 'There was something going on in the City today, and from the excitement I hope it is good news. There have been rumours of a great battle and a retreat, but that was not the mood I detected today. But I cannot understand why no one at the Foreign Office seems to be aware of it.'

'We will hear soon enough,' she said calmly. 'Tell me about your friend. When was he wounded? Has he completely recovered? Has he been married long?'

★ ★ ★

The ballroom was at the back of the house, but it was hot from the heat of hundreds of candles, the windows had been opened, and Julia was thankful to step out on to one of the balconies for a breath of air. She turned to smile at Sir Carey as he followed her.

'Are you feeling faint?' he asked. 'Do you wish for a glass of wine?'

'That would be welcome, though I am not feeling faint, just hot. Wait. Listen,' she added as he made to step back into the ballroom. 'What's that noise?'

They could hear cheering, coming closer, and gradually the chanting of hundreds of voices.

'Boney's beat! Boney's beat!'

'It's the news, it must be,' Julia said.

Other people had heard it too, and there was a sudden stampede as the guests rushed for the door on to St James's Square. Sir Carey seized Julia's hand and they joined the exodus. As they reached the square a large chaise went past, drawn by four horses and decked with laurels. Out of the windows hung three Imperial Eagles, and the French colours.

'We've won! Wellington has triumphed,' the crowd cheered.

The chaise stopped further round the square, and a man alighted and ran up to the front door.

'That looks like Mrs Boehm's house,' Sir Carey said. 'I heard some of the Cabinet were dining there tonight.'

Faint cheers came from the house, and soon the crowd of people already in the square were joined by others who had seen the coach and followed it, desperate for news. Julia looked round. There were many of the *ton* in evening dress, servants from the houses round about, hackney coachmen and link boys, and some of the prostitutes who plied their trade in Piccadilly. They crowded round the chaise, trying to touch the colours, and begging for news.

'A great victory!' the cry went up.

'Are there any casualty lists?' an elderly man near Julia was demanding urgently, and she turned to look at his haggard face.

Many of the other people crowding round the chaise were also anxiously demanding news, but there was none. Battles meant deaths, she reminded herself, and turned away. Sir Carey put his arm round her shoulders and led her away.

'We'll hear more in the morning,' he said quietly. 'Shall we go home now?'

Julia nodded. Despite the relief of hearing news of the victory, it was tempered by the distress that would be felt by all those who had loved ones in the army, and who might not know for days whether they were safe, wounded or killed.

She slept little that night, and wished she could have been comforted by Sir Carey's arms around her, and perhaps have comforted him. She knew no one in the army, but he must have known many fellow soldiers, some of them friends, and be wondering about their fates.

In the morning Sir Carey went early to the Foreign Office, then returned to escort Julia to the parade on the Mall.

'One of Nathaniel Rothschild's men heard the news, in Belgium, and rode to London, beating the official messenger. That explains the excitement in the City,' he told her.

'Was the battle bad?' Julia asked.

'There were many casualties,' he said. They were walking towards the parade ground, having decided it would probably be too crowded for a carriage. 'We haven't many details yet, apart from what the messenger knows. It was a brief note only, Wellington was too exhausted to write much, I understand.'

'That is not surprising.'

The parade ground was crowded, and the windows and roofs of every house overlooking it were crowded with people. Julia had to blink back tears when a man in a bloodstained uniform alighted from a coach and was greeted by the Duke of York. The crowd cheered wildly, and the band began to play *See the Conquering Hero Comes*.

'That's Henry Percy, ADC to Wellington,' Sir Carey told her. 'It's said he delivered the dispatches to Lord Liverpool and the Prince Regent last night, and was instantly promoted to colonel. We'll hear more news over the next few days.'

17

Sir Carey was thankful to be going home to Courtlands. They were taking the large travelling coach, as well as a separate one for the baggage and the servants, which they had sent on ahead, for they had a great deal of luggage. He would not be needing it for some time, he decided, as neither he nor Julia wished to return to the Continent. Julia had been busy purchasing fabrics for the new curtains, and when Sir Carey saw how much room these parcels took up, as well as the trunks of clothes, he elected to ride. He needed time to think. The arrangements Lord Castlereagh had worked for in Vienna would hold, now Napoleon was once more defeated and had again abdicated, though as yet he had not been captured. He would probably be sent to a far-distant place. He was no more a threat, and he could look forward to the birthday celebrations Julia was busily planning for the middle of the month.

They had decided to hold this at Courtlands, where all his tenants, the villagers, and local squires could attend. 'For they know you well, and are more important than the people we know in London,' Julia had said. He smiled in appreciation. It was what he wished, but if Angelica had been in charge she would have wanted a large party in London, to show off to as many people as they could accommodate. He smiled. Most people would have gone to Brighton or some other seaside resort by mid-July, so attendance would have been sparse.

Angelica had been taken home in disgrace after her latest escapade. Perhaps, he hoped, she had ceased her pursuit of him. If, as she had claimed, his attraction had been his half-ruined castle, then she would soon turn her attention to some other unfortunate owner. If that had been mere bravado, she was young enough to get over any affection she felt for him, especially after the brutal dressing down he had given her. He gave thanks, as he frequently now did, that he had escaped her and instead found his Julia. He thought back reminiscently. He had liked Julia in Vienna, enjoyed her company, but felt no more than liking for her then. It had been a marriage of convenience, when he had been sure he would never be able to love another woman. Why had he promised her he would make no other demands?

Gradually, as they had spent more time together on the journey, and she took charge of his home and sisters, he had come to love her. He looked forward to spending the rest of his life with her. He wanted to have children like her, but in view of his promise how could he ask to share her bed? Unless she wanted it too, and she had given no sign of that, he could not suggest it. She might think she had to agree, and would feel cheated as she had been promised it would be a marriage in name only.

They were within a dozen miles of home, and riding through a densely wooded stretch of road when his musings were abruptly cut short. A hoarse voice coming from the far side of the coach shouted something, and a shot whistled past the ear of Frisby, on the box. Startled, Frisby pulled on the reins and the coach came to a ragged halt.

The voice was nearer now, demanding money and jewels. Sir Carey drew his own pistols from the holsters, and edged towards the back of the coach. It was just one horseman, he decided, and nudged his horse forward. The man, a hat pulled down over his eyes and a heavy muffler round his face, was on a thin black horse, and pointing a pistol at the coach window.

'Out, woman, and bring all they valuables wi' ye.'

'Drop that pistol, you are covered!' Sir

Carey ordered, riding round to the side of the coach.

With an oath the highwayman swung round, and his pistol went off as Sir Carey fired. The man dropped his pistol and clutched his arm, and unable to keep his balance as the black horse reared in fright, fell heavily to the ground.

Sir Carey ignored him and threw himself at the coach door, dragging it open. If Julia had been hurt, even killed, he would never forgive himself.

She was sitting in the far corner, deathly white, an arm red with blood held in front of her. He scrambled into the coach.

'Julia, my love, where were you hit?'

She looked down at her arm. 'I — just my arm. I think it is just a flesh wound. I can still move it,' she said, sounding surprised.

'Let me see.'

He tore off his cravat, then with a pocket knife gently cut away the sleeve of her travelling gown to reveal an ugly gash just below her shoulder.

'His aim went wild when you shouted,' she explained, her voice trembling. 'He was pointing directly at my heart.'

Sir Carey breathed a sigh of relief. He'd been terrified his intervention had caused the man to fire.

'As you say, a flesh wound,' he said, trying to keep his voice calm. 'I'll bind it up for now, and then we'll find the nearest inn and you can rest.'

'No, please. Let's go home. It's not far, and I'd much rather be in my own bed.'

He was about to argue when Frisby's face appeared at the window.

'Is her ladyship hurt?' the coachman asked. 'I've tied the rogue up. He stunned hisself when he fell off the nag. It's Samuel, sir.'

★ ★ ★

Julia, though pale, insisted on remaining in the stable yard while Sir Carey questioned their erstwhile groom. He had recovered his senses soon after they had thrown him into the coach, and she and Sir Carey, who hitched both horses to the back while he rode inside with Julia, had been forced to listen to his imprecations. His arm had been broken by Sir Carey's bullet, and Sir Carey had fashioned a rough bandage with a strip torn off Samuel's shirt, and a sling with his muffler.

'I'll call the doctor when you tell me who set you up,' Sir Carey told him, 'so the longer you refuse to speak the worse it will be for you.'

Samuel, with a shrug, gave in. 'If I tells yer, do I get special treatment?'

'Transportation instead of the gallows? That will be up to the magistrates.'

The man seemed resigned. 'It were Mr Fitzhugh,' he said. 'When 'e heard you was wed he sent me ter get rid of the jade. I paid one of yer grooms ter leave, an' got 'is job.'

'And tried to murder my wife by pushing a rock from the battlements.'

'That were just an impulse, yer might say. I dain't think it'ld work. But the girths should 'ave.'

He sounded resentful, and despite the pain in her arm and the horror of knowing for certain that someone had tried to kill her, Julia could not suppress a chuckle.

'So you thought your pistol would be more certain, did you?' she asked.

'I thought both of yer would be in the coach,' he muttered. 'When's this plaguey sawbones comin', me arm's real bad?'

'He's been sent for, but you'll have to wait until he's attended to Lady Evelegh. Make sure he doesn't escape,' Sir Carey ordered the grooms and gardeners he'd summoned as soon as they arrived home.

'No one who tries to murder our mistress gets away with it,' the head groom said, and Julia felt a glow of pleasure that they all seemed determined to avenge her.

She allowed Sir Carey to lead her away, and was thankful he brushed aside the anxious enquiries of the indoor servants as he led her up to her bedroom. He would have carried her, but she insisted she was able to walk. She was unutterably glad to sink down on to the bed, however.

Molly had followed them in. 'Shall I take your gown off, my lady?' the maid asked.

Sir Carey, after a slight hesitation, nodded. 'I think that's the doctor I can hear now. I'll go and bring him up.'

* * *

The following day Sir Carey set off for Lincolnshire. Samuel had been taken to Oxford gaol, and Julia, though pale, had insisted she was well enough to be left. A shocked and penitent Caroline, weeping copiously and apologizing for her behaviour in London, declared she would not leave Julia's side and would perform whatever services were necessary.

'For I don't want Carey to divorce you,' she said tearfully. 'I was furious you'd found me at the masquerade, and when Angelica suggested I let her into the house I just thought it was a lark. I really wouldn't like her as my stepsister, ordering me about,' she added, and Sir Carey had to stifle a laugh.

The journey he was going on was not amusing. He drove post, going first to London to make sure Daniel was not there, insisting that Daniel's attorney accompanied him, then taking the Great North Road.

He arrived at Daniel's house late at night, having booked rooms at the village inn and left an exhausted attorney, to whom he had explained the whole, there. He was so angry he did not want to leave his encounter until morning.

A wary butler opened the door to him. The man had been in service with Daniel for many years, and recognized Sir Carey, so opened the door wide and let him in. A tabby cat, watching for the opportunity, shot out of the door just before it was closed again.

'Sir Carey! We weren't expecting you. I can order a room for you.'

'Don't bother, I won't be sleeping here. Where is your master?'

The man gestured towards a door at the back of the hall and Sir Carey walked straight in, not waiting to be announced. It was a billiard room and Daniel was just taking a shot as the door opened. He started, and the shot went wide.

'Damn you, can't you knock?' he snarled,

then looked up and saw it was Sir Carey. 'What the devil brings you here?'

'To report the failure of your latest attempt to murder my wife.'

'Murder? What are you talking about?' Daniel put down his cue and stooping, picked up another cat, this time a large ginger animal with only one ear.

'Your man Samuel has confessed, so you need not plead ignorance. Three times he has tried to murder Julia, but he's now awaiting trial and he'll be fortunate to escape with his own life. He'll implicate you as well. Tell me, Daniel, why did you bother? I'm married, and the will is clear, Grandfather's money comes to me.'

Daniel looked as though he wanted to deny it, but shrugged. 'The will says you need to be married on your thirtieth birthday, not before it. If I got rid of her, all would be well.'

'I see.' Sir Carey sat down on one of the benches that ran down the two long sides of the room, and absently began to stroke the cat, this time a black and white one, that immediately sprang on to his lap. 'Whether a court would make the same interpretation is doubtful. Were you and your despicable ally in Yorkshire trying to remove Angelica permanently, or just until after my birthday?' he asked.

'Oh, just temporarily,' he admitted. 'You could have enjoyed her afterwards, but instead you made this crazy marriage to an unknown chit. I should have sent Samuel to kill you,' he went on, 'but somehow I could not bring myself to dispose of my own flesh and blood.'

Sir Carey shivered. 'I'm not sure I want to claim the relationship.'

'What are you going to do?' Daniel asked. 'Is it to be pistols at dawn?'

'Oh, I don't think so. If I were in the habit of issuing challenges, it would only be to honourable gentlemen. You deserve to be thrown into Newgate, but I don't want my name, and that of my wife, dragged through the courts. For Samuel, we can ensure there is little publicity. He's just one more highwayman. But if you don't accept my suggestion I am prepared to face that.'

'Your suggestion?'

'Of course. You don't imagine I am going to forgive and forget this, do you? I want you far away from Julia. In America or Australia, you may choose.'

'Emigrate?' For the first time Daniel showed some agitation. 'I don't want to leave England, leave my cats!'

'You would have to leave them if you went to Newgate,' Sir Carey pointed out. 'Your man of business can deal with selling your property in England, and send on the proceeds. I think you could buy many square miles of land in either country with that money. I'm prepared to advance you five thousand pounds against the sale, so that you can buy a house and look around you as soon as you get there.'

'I don't want to leave England!'

Sir Carey rose to his feet, dislodging a disgruntled cat. 'Then I must apply to the magistrate here and lay charges.'

'Wait! How can you expect me to make up my mind in such a hurry?'

'I'd have thought there was little choice. You go of your own free will, to a country you choose, instead of being transported in chains as a convict.'

Daniel was pacing the room, frowning.

'You might even take your cats,' Sir Carey suggested. 'Your attorney is at the village inn, and I will bring him here in the morning so that you can give him your instructions. He knows everything, by the way.'

'Damn you! You leave me no choice, but I won't go to Australia where most of the population are criminals! I'll go to Canada.'

★ ★ ★

Julia tossed and turned, despite all Molly could do to soothe her. The wound in her arm was not mending as quickly as she had expected, and she was often delirious. Where was Sir Carey? Why did he not come to her? They told her he had gone away, but was expected back hourly. Sometimes she dreamed he was there in the room with her, but when she awoke and had lucid periods, he was never there. She obediently swallowed the medicine the doctor brought, and suffered the repeated applications of poultices to her inflamed arm.

It was a week after the shooting when she had a more vivid dream than usual. She thought Sir Carey was sitting on the bed beside her, holding her uninjured hand.

'Oh, I thought you would never come,' she murmured. 'Kiss me. I need you, Carey my love. Don't ever leave me again, I love you so.'

She began to sob. Someone stroked her forehead, pushing her hair back, and she tried to take hold of the hand. Then she felt a cool kiss on her cheek, and with a gasp turned her head so that her lips met his. It was Sir Carey, she knew it, and with a sigh she quietened.

Some time later she awoke, lucid, and recalled the dream. It had been the most vivid yet, and she became hot at the recollection of what she had said. She glanced round, but the room was empty. She hoped no one had been present to hear her ramblings. It was too embarrassing.

Shortly afterwards Molly came in with a tray. 'You're awake, my lady, and looking better. The doctor's here, and when he's dressed your arm you can have a light meal. There's chicken broth and a boiled egg.'

'I feel stronger,' Julia said, 'and I'm tired of invalid food. I'd like some slices of ham, and a peach if there are any in the hothouses.'

'Good, you are better,' Molly said. 'I'll see about it when the doctor has finished.'

Julia felt well, apart from the soreness in her arm, and the doctor nodded in approval when he poulticed it.

'Good, the poison has been drawn out, and it's healing well now. There may be a slight scar, but it's high on the arm, almost on the shoulder, and your gowns will cover it.'

She was ravenous, and ate the ham and some thin slices of chicken breast Molly brought, followed by a large, ripe peach. Then she slid down under the covers again, saying she was tired and would sleep. Molly smiled, tucked the covers round her, drew the curtains, and slipped out of the room. Wondering whether she would be strong enough to get up for a few hours on the following day and begin on the preparations for Sir Carey's birthday celebrations, she fell asleep.

* * *

Sir Carey was smiling as he rode round the farms. It was the first opportunity he'd had, as he had left for Lincolnshire the moment Samuel had been taken off to gaol, and since his return the previous day had spent much of the time sitting beside Julia. Now she seemed on the mend, from the doctor's report, and the news Molly brought that she had recovered her appetite.

He knew now that she loved him. The problem would be to convince her he had fallen in love with her too. But he didn't doubt his ability to do that. He would need to wait until she recovered her strength, perhaps until after his birthday, which was just a week away.

He had not expected to fall in love. It was a totally different emotion to the one he'd felt for Angelica. That had been infatuation. If he believed in witchcraft he'd have thought the girl had bewitched him. He'd been dazzled by her beauty, and her obvious adoration of him. Her beauty would probably fade in time, and long before that he would have been bored and irritated by her shallow nature. Julia was beautiful in a different, quieter, but more lasting way. She had a strength of character he could not recall ever finding in other women. She was brave, resourceful, and had already made his life more comfortable than he could remember. But none of these qualities mattered. He simply loved her and wanted to spend the rest of his life with her.

When he reached home late in the afternoon he found Julia sitting in the library, surrounded by lists. She looked up with a smile.

'Is all well on the farms?' she asked.

'It is. But should you be up, my dear?'

'I mean to go back to bed straight after dinner, but I wanted to leave my room for a time. I feel so much better. Molly tells me you have been away. Is it Lord Castlereagh? Are there problems in Belgium? I have heard no news.'

'No, the armies have entered Paris. I went to Lincolnshire, on private business. With Daniel.'

She looked at him, raising her eyebrows.

'He admitted he sent Samuel here to murder you.' He paused. Even now the thought of Daniel's activities made him furious. 'I gave him an ultimatum. He either left England for somewhere far away, or I turned him over to the authorities. He chose

318

to go to Canada, and his attorney will sell his property here, so I doubt he'll want to return.'

'What about his cats?' Julia asked, and chuckled. 'Did you see them?'

He grinned at the recollection. When he had finally left Daniel the morning after their confrontation, and after the attorney had finished his business, the man had been trying to collect his cats in one room, ready for confining in cages so that they could be taken to the ship. Every time he had captured one and opened the door to push it in, another feline had escaped, and Daniel had suffered several scratches on his hands.

'Too many.' He told Julia of Daniel's struggles and she gurgled with delight.

'So he is safely out of the country.'

'He will be in a few days. I booked a passage on a ship from Liverpool; it sails next week. But enough of him. What have you planned for my birthday?'

★ ★ ★

Julia surveyed the shambles on the lawn in front of the house. The trestle tables still held some food, though most of the pies, the meats which had been roasted, including a whole pig and several sheep, plus a side of beef and numerous fowls, had been eaten, along with the soft white loaves. The pastries and other sweetmeats had been demolished, and the barrels of ale and cider were almost empty.

The jugglers and acrobats Elizabeth had sent down from London at Julia's request were packing their equipment into a large cart. Musicians recruited by Foster from the villages nearby were scraping on their fiddles for a country dance, and most of the guests, apart from the very young and the old, were singing as they danced.

Julia, pleading her recent illness, had declined, and was sitting on a stool watching Sir Carey partnering the buxom Mrs Harris while her son Jed bashfully led Caroline down the line as it became their turn.

The local squires and their wives had been invited to dinner, and Julia had arranged for another buffet to be set up in the dining room. The servants had been working non-stop for several days to prepare all the food, and she wanted them to be free to enjoy their own festivities, not have to wait at table.

The informality seemed appreciated by her guests. By now she knew most of them, she and Sir Carey had dined with them, or they had come to her dinner party before she went to London. A few had also been in London, and they had met at balls and assemblies there.

'A wonderful day,' one of the older men said to her. 'Carey's a lucky young devil to have captured you, my dear.'

Eventually they took their leave, and Julia forbade the servants from clearing up that evening.

'It's late, and you must be longing for your beds,' she told them firmly.

They bade her a good night and dispersed. Sir Carey was locking the doors and windows, and Julia said a brief goodnight to him and went wearily upstairs. She was tired, but she knew she would not sleep.

She was sitting by her window watching the last of the sunset when the door of her room opened. Thinking it was Molly she did not turn round. 'I told you all to go to bed,' she said. 'I can do for myself tonight.'

'But I'd rather help you.'

She swung round to see Sir Carey standing in the doorway carrying a bottle of champagne and two glasses. He came into the room and set them down on a small table near the bed. He had removed his coat and waistcoat, and she could see his rippling muscles under the shirt and pantaloons.

'I . . . what do you mean?' she asked, breathless.

He came across and pulled her to her feet. 'Thank you for the best birthday of my life,' he said, and took her in his arms, bending to capture her lips with his own. 'Julia,' he said, as they broke apart, 'I want you to release me from my promise.'

'What promise?'

'That I would not expect a proper marriage. But I have grown to love you dearly, and from what you said when you were delirious, I think you could come to love me too.'

Julia thought back and blushed. She was recalling her dream that she had told him she loved him. 'It was a dream!' she exclaimed.

He laughed. 'You may have thought so, but I did not imagine it. You did not know what you were saying, but I know it was the truth. Julia, could you love me?'

She nodded, unable to speak. This was a dream come true. With a satisfied sigh he drew her into his arms again, and kissed her long and deeply. As they broke apart he pulled the pins out of her hair and let it ripple over his hands. She was wearing a simple muslin gown, fastened with strings round the neck. He pulled the strings free, and slid the gown down over her body. Swiftly he divested himself of his clothes and before Julia knew it she was lying in his arms. He caressed her gently, murmuring how much he wanted her, kissing her until she was desperate for more, and when she thought she could bear it no longer he entered her, and it was the most exquisite sensation she had ever known.

Hours later, it seemed to Julia, he sat up and reached for the champagne. Quickly he released the cork and poured the bubbling wine into the glasses. He handed one to her, and took the other, raising it in salute.

'To Julia, my dearest love, and the best birthday present I have ever had.'

She sighed with pleasure. 'I think it may already be the day after your birthday, Carey.'

'We will stop the clocks. But now, sweetheart, we can pretend it's a birthday every day. In case I didn't say, I love you dearly. I was so fortunate to find you on that Bavarian road. It was an odd marriage, but the best one I could ever have made.'

'For me too,' she whispered, and he set down the glasses and reached for her.

'We'll start the clocks again in — oh, a year's time?' he suggested, and she laughed, and went to him.

We do hope that you have enjoyed reading this large print book.

Did you know that all of our titles are available for purchase?

We publish a wide range of high quality large print books including:
Romances, Mysteries, Classics
General Fiction
Non Fiction and Westerns

Special interest titles available in large print are:
The Little Oxford Dictionary
Music Book
Song Book
Hymn Book
Service Book

Also available from us courtesy of Oxford University Press:
Young Readers' Dictionary
(large print edition)
Young Readers' Thesaurus
(large print edition)

For further information or a free brochure, please contact us at:
Ulverscroft Large Print Books Ltd.,
The Green, Bradgate Road, Anstey,
Leicester, LE7 7FU, England.
Tel: (00 44) 0116 236 4325
Fax: (00 44) 0116 234 0205

Other titles published by
The House of Ulverscroft:

CAMPAIGN FOR A BRIDE

Marina Oliver

Arranged marriages were common in the seventeenth century, and Barbara was married to Ludovick when she was still a child. Ludovick then spent the next few years fighting for the King. When Barbara is grown up, she is confronted with the prospect of this virtually unknown husband's return. By now the marriage is hateful to her, for she has fallen in love with her brother's friend, Nigel. They run away together — but Ludovick is not prepared to let Barbara go so easily.

MASQUERADE FOR THE KING

Marina Oliver

Tavern wench Sanchia could not easily be forgotten. Royalist Sir John Morriss and the arrogant Comte de St. Etienne are both taken by her. Sanchia, forced to flee from the inn which has given her refuge and employment, joins those working for the Restoration of Charles. Unexpected danger and uncertainty loom for both Sanchia and the King, and as the King triumphs, Sanchia's own future is also secured.

RUNAWAY HILL

Marina Oliver

When the dashing Sir Randal Thornton aids Drusilla during the Parliamentary siege of Reading, she realises how foolish she is to fall in love with him. Especially since her brother is fighting for Parliament, and was one of the deputation which protested about the King's Ship Money tax. But having glimpsed the possibility of happiness, she is even more determined to marry for love.

CAVALIER COURTSHIP

Marina Oliver

Headstrong Caroline, a secret supporter of the Royalist cause, dreamed of helping the King. Brought up by a Puritan uncle, life in his household became intolerable. Ill-treated, dispossessed and threatened with marriage, she looked for a means of escape, becoming involved in the intrigues of the Royalists during the last months of Cromwell's protectorate. But she is also haunted by the shadow of a sinister Roundhead Colonel, who desires her, but also threatens her safety.

THE DREADFUL DUKE

Barbara Hazard

There seemed no reason why Lady Juliet Manchester should not be wed. She was beautiful, charming and intelligent. But this Juliet allowed no male to play Romeo to her. The reasons she kept to herself, but no man would ever have her as a wife. The Duke of Severn was never denied or defeated: his wishes were others' commands, and society's most ravishing belles were his for the asking. It was unthinkable that Juliet could resist his advances or refuse his proposal. But when this iron-willed lord attempted to storm the defences of this unyielding lady, the unthinkable did happen.

MISS PRESTWICK'S CRUSADE

Anne Barbour

Miss Helen Prestwick has arrived in England from Portugal, to secure the future of her nephew, the twelfth Earl of Camberwell. Lacking evidence that the child is the son of Christopher Beresford who died in battle, her claim will enrage Christopher's cousin Edward, who currently wields the title. After his cousin's death Edward Beresford had never wanted the earldom, but he's not going to surrender the title without verifying the legitimacy of Helen's claim. However, Edward finds himself enchanted with the child's lovely guardian, whose mission to usurp his title has also ensnared his heart.